Tuck Everlasting

Natalie Babbitt

••••

With
Connected Readings

PRENTICE HALL
Upper Saddle River, New Jersey
Needham, Massachusetts

ISBN 0-13-437487-8

6 7 8 9 10   03 02 01

PRENTICE HALL

Acknowledgments

Grateful acknowledgment is made to the following for permission to reprint copyrighted material:

Don Congdon Associates, Inc.
"The Happiness Machine" by Ray Bradbury. Originally published in *The Saturday Evening Post,* September 14, 1957. Copyright © 1957 by the Curtis Publishing Co., renewed 1985 by Ray Bradbury. Reprinted by permission of Don Congdon Associates, Inc.

Farrar, Straus & Giroux, Inc.
Tuck Everlasting by Natalie Babbitt. Copyright © 1975 by Natalie Babbitt. All rights reserved. Published by arrangement with Farrar, Straus & Giroux, Inc. Excerpt from *The Eyes of the Amaryllis* by Natalie Babbitt. Copyright © 1977 by Natalie Babbitt. All rights reserved. Reprinted by permission of Farrar, Straus & Giroux, Inc.

Houghton Mifflin Company
Excerpt from *The Giver* by Lois Lowry. Copyright © 1993 by Lois Lowry. Reprinted by permission of Houghton Mifflin Company. All rights reserved.

Little, Brown and Company
"Peekaboo, I Almost See You" from *Verses from 1929 On* by Ogden Nash. Copyright © 1949 by Ogden Nash; copyright © renewed 1976 by Frances Nash, Isabel Nash Eberstadt, and Linnell Nash Smith, first published in *The Saturday Evening Post.* By permission of Little, Brown and Company.

Millbrook Press
Excerpt from *Virtual Reality: A Door to Cyberspace* by Ann E. Weiss. Text copyright © 1996 by Ann E. Weiss. Reprinted by permission of Millbrook Press.

Newsweek
"John Glenn, Time Traveler" by Matt Bai, from *Newsweek,* October 26, 1998, © 1998 Newsweek, Inc. All rights reserved. Reprinted by permission of *Newsweek.*

(Acknowledgments continue on p. 128)

Contents

Tuck Everlasting

Tuck Everlasting

Natalie Babbitt

Prologue

THE first week of August hangs at the very top of summer, the top of the live-long year, like the highest seat of a Ferris wheel when it pauses in its turning. The weeks that come before are only a climb from balmy spring, and those that follow a drop to the chill of autumn, but the first week of August is motionless, and hot. It is curiously silent, too, with blank white dawns and glaring noons, and sunsets smeared with too much color. Often at night there is lightning, but it quivers all alone. There is no thunder, no relieving rain. These are strange and breathless days, the dog days, when people are led to do things they are sure to be sorry for after.

One day at that time, not so very long ago, three things happened and at first there appeared to be no connection between them.

At dawn, Mae Tuck set out on her horse for the wood at the edge of the village of Treegap. She was going there, as she did once every ten years, to meet her two sons, Miles and Jesse.

At noontime, Winnie Foster, whose family owned the Treegap wood, lost her patience at last and decided to think about running away.

And at sunset a stranger appeared at the Fosters' gate. He was looking for someone, but he didn't say who.

No connection, you would agree. But things can come together in strange ways. The wood was at the center, the hub of the wheel. All wheels must have a hub. A Ferris wheel has one, as the sun is the hub of the wheeling calendar. Fixed points they are, and best left undisturbed, for without them, nothing holds together. But sometimes people find this out too late.

Chapter 1

THE road that led to Treegap had been trod out long before by a herd of cows who were, to say the least, relaxed. It wandered along in curves and easy angles, swayed off and up in a pleasant tangent to the top of a small hill, ambled down again between fringes of bee-hung clover, and then cut sidewise across a meadow. Here its edges blurred. It widened and seemed to pause, suggesting tranquil bovine picnics: slow chewing and thoughtful contemplation of the infinite. And then it went on again and came at last to the wood. But on reaching the shadows of the first trees, it veered sharply, swung out in a wide arc as if, for the first time, it had reason to think where it was going, and passed around.

On the other side of the wood, the sense of easiness dissolved. The road no longer belonged to the cows. It became, instead, and rather abruptly, the property of people. And all at once the sun was uncomfortably hot, the dust oppressive, and the meager grass along its edges somewhat ragged and forlorn. On the left stood the first house, a square and solid cottage with a touch-me-not appearance, surrounded by grass cut painfully to the quick and enclosed by a capable iron fence some four feet high which clearly said, "Move on—we don't want *you* here." So the road went humbly by and made its way, past cottages more and more frequent but less and less forbidding, into the village. But the village doesn't matter, except for the jailhouse and the gallows. The first house only is important; the first house, the road, and the wood.

There was something strange about the wood. If the look of the first house suggested that you'd better pass it by, so did the look of the wood, but for quite a different reason. The house was so proud of itself that you wanted to make a lot of noise as you passed, and maybe even throw a rock or two. But the wood had a sleeping, otherworld appearance that made you want to speak in whispers. This, at least, is what the cows must have thought: "Let it keep its peace; *we* won't disturb it."

Whether the people felt that way about the wood or not is difficult to say. There were some, perhaps, who did. But for the most part the people followed the road around the wood because that was the way it led. There was no road *through* the wood. And anyway, for the people, there was another reason to leave the wood to itself: it belonged to the Fosters, the owners of the touch-me-not cottage, and was therefore private property in spite of the fact that it lay outside the fence and was perfectly accessible.

The ownership of land is an odd thing when you come to think of it. How deep, after all, can it go? If a person owns a piece of land, does he own it all the way down, in ever narrowing dimensions, till it meets all other pieces at the center of the earth? Or does ownership consist only of a thin crust under which the friendly worms have never heard of trespassing?

In any case, the wood, being on top—except, of course, for its roots—was owned bud and bough by the Fosters in the touch-me-not cottage, and if they never went there, if they never wandered in among the trees, well, that was their affair. Winnie, the only child of the house, never went there, though she sometimes stood inside the fence, carelessly banging a stick against the iron bars, and looked at it. But she had never been curious about it. Nothing ever seems interesting when it belongs to you—only when it doesn't.

And what is interesting, anyway, about a slim few acres of trees? There will be a dimness shot through with bars of sunlight, a great many squirrels and birds, a deep, damp mattress of leaves on the ground, and all the other things just as familiar if not so pleasant—things like spiders, thorns, and grubs.

In the end, however, it was the cows who were responsible for the wood's isolation, and the cows, through some wisdom they were not wise enough to know that they possessed, were very wise indeed. If they had made their road through the wood instead of around it, then the people would have followed the road. The people would have noticed the giant ash tree at the center of the wood, and then, in time, they'd have noticed the little spring bubbling up among its roots in spite of the pebbles piled there to conceal it. And that would have been a disaster so immense that this weary old earth, owned or not to its fiery core, would have trembled on its axis like a beetle on a pin.

Chapter 2

AND so, at dawn, that day in the first week of August, Mae Tuck woke up and lay for a while beaming at the cobwebs on the ceiling. At last she said aloud, "The boys'll be home tomorrow!"

Mae's husband, on his back beside her, did not stir. He was still asleep, and the melancholy creases that folded his daytime face were smoothed and slack. He snored gently, and for a moment the corners of his mouth turned upward in a smile. Tuck almost never smiled except in sleep.

Mae sat up in bed and looked at him tolerantly. "The boys'll be home tomorrow," she said again, a little more loudly.

Tuck twitched and the smile vanished. He opened his eyes. "Why'd you have to wake me up?" he sighed. "I was having that dream again, the good one where we're all in heaven and never heard of Treegap."

Mae sat there frowning, a great potato of a woman with a round, sensible face and calm brown eyes. "It's no use having that dream," she said. "Nothing's going to change."

"You tell me that every day," said Tuck, turning away from her onto his side. "Anyways, I can't help what I dream."

"Maybe not," said Mae. "But, all the same, you should've got used to things by now."

Tuck groaned. "I'm going back to sleep," he said.

"Not me," said Mae. "I'm going to take the horse and go down to the wood to meet them."

"Meet who?"

"The boys, Tuck! Our sons. I'm going to ride down to meet them."

"Better not do that," said Tuck.

"I know," said Mae, "but I just can't wait to see them. Anyways, it's ten years since I went to Treegap. No one'll remember me. I'll ride in at sunset, just to the wood. I won't go into the village. But, even if someone did see me, they won't remember. They never did before, now, did they?"

"Suit yourself, then," said Tuck into his pillow. "I'm going back to sleep."

Mae Tuck climbed out of bed and began to dress: three petticoats, a rusty brown skirt with one enormous pocket, an old cotton jacket, and a knitted shawl which she pinned across her bosom with a tarnished metal brooch. The sounds of her dressing were so familiar to Tuck that he could say, without opening his eyes, "You don't need that shawl in the middle of the summer."

Mae ignored this observation. Instead, she said, "Will you be all right? We won't get back till late tomorrow."

Tuck rolled over and made a rueful face at her. "What in the world could possibly happen to me?"

"That's so," said Mae. "I keep forgetting."

"*I* don't," said Tuck. "Have a nice time." And in a moment he was asleep again.

Mae sat on the edge of the bed and pulled on a pair of short leather boots so thin and soft with age it was a wonder they held together. Then she stood and took from the washstand beside the bed a little square-shaped object, a music box painted with roses and lilies of the valley. It was the one pretty thing she owned and she never went anywhere without it. Her fingers strayed to the winding key on its bottom, but glancing at the sleeping Tuck, she shook her head, gave the little box a pat, and dropped it into her pocket. Then, last of all, she pulled down over her ears a blue straw hat with a drooping, exhausted brim.

But, before she put on the hat, she brushed her gray-brown hair and wound it into a bun at the back of her neck. She did this quickly and skillfully without a single glance in the mirror. Mae Tuck didn't need a mirror, though she had one propped up on the washstand. She knew very well what she would see in it; her reflection had long since ceased to interest her. For Mae Tuck, and her husband, and Miles and Jesse, too, had all looked exactly the same for eighty-seven years.

Chapter 3

AT noon of that same day in the first week of August, Winnie Foster sat on the bristly grass just inside the fence and said to the large toad who was squatting a few yards away across the road, "I will, though. You'll see. Maybe even first thing tomorrow, while everyone's still asleep."

It was hard to know whether the toad was listening or not. Certainly, Winnie had given it good reason to ignore her. She had come out to the fence, very cross, very near the boiling point on a day that was itself near to boiling, and had noticed the toad at once. It was the only living thing in sight except for a stationary cloud of hysterical gnats suspended in the heat above the road. Winnie had found some pebbles at the base of the fence and, for lack of any other way to show how she felt, had flung one at the toad. It missed altogether, as she'd fully intended it should, but she made a game of it anyway, tossing pebbles at such an angle that they passed through the gnat cloud on their way to the toad. The gnats were too frantic to notice these intrusions, however, and since every pebble missed its final mark, the toad continued to squat and grimace without so much as a twitch. Possibly it felt resentful. Or perhaps it was only asleep. In either case, it gave her not a glance when at last she ran out of pebbles and sat down to tell it her troubles.

"Look here, toad," she said, thrusting her arms through the bars of the fence and plucking at the weeds on the other side. "I don't think I can stand it much longer."

At this moment a window at the front of the cottage was flung open and a thin voice—her grandmother's—piped, "Winifred! Don't sit on that dirty grass. You'll stain your boots and stockings."

And another, firmer voice—her mother's—added, "Come in now, Winnie. Right away. You'll get heat stroke out there on a day like this. And your lunch is ready."

"See?" said Winnie to the toad. "That's just what I mean. It's like that every minute. If I had a sister or a brother, there'd be someone else for them to watch. But, as it is, there's only me. I'm tired of being looked at all the time. I want to be by myself for a change." She leaned her forehead against the bars and after a short silence went on in a thoughtful tone. "I'm not exactly sure what I'd do, you know, but something interesting—something that's all mine. Something that would make some kind of difference in the world. It'd be nice to have a new name, to start with, one that's not all worn out from being called so much. And I might even decide to have a pet. Maybe a big old toad, like you, that I could keep in a nice cage with lots of grass, and . . ."

At this the toad stirred and blinked. It gave a heave of muscles and plopped its heavy mudball of a body a few inches farther away from her.

"I suppose you're right," said Winnie. "Then you'd be just the way I am, now. Why should you have to be cooped up in a cage, too? It'd be better if I could be like you, out in the open and making up my own mind. Do you know they've hardly ever let me out of this yard all by myself? I'll never be able to do anything important if I stay in here like this. I expect I'd better run away." She paused and peered anxiously at the toad to see how it would receive this staggering idea, but it showed no signs of interest. "You think I wouldn't dare, don't you?" she said accusingly. "I will, though. You'll see. Maybe even first thing in the morning, while everyone's still asleep."

"Winnie!" came the firm voice from the window.

"All *right!* I'm coming!" she cried, exasperated, and then added quickly, "I mean, I'll be right there, Mama." She stood up, brushing at her legs where bits of itchy grass clung to her stockings.

The toad, as if it saw that their interview was over, stirred again, bunched up, and bounced itself clumsily off toward the wood. Winnie watched it go. "Hop away, toad," she called after it. "You'll see. Just wait till morning."

Chapter 4

AT sunset of that same long day, a stranger came strolling up the road from the village and paused at the Fosters' gate. Winnie

8

was once again in the yard, this time intent on catching fireflies, and at first she didn't notice him. But, after a few moments of watching her, he called out, "Good evening!"

He was remarkably tall and narrow, this stranger standing there. His long chin faded off into a thin, apologetic beard, but his suit was a jaunty yellow that seemed to glow a little in the fading light. A black hat dangled from one hand, and as Winnie came toward him, he passed the other through his dry, gray hair, settling it smoothly. "Well, now," he said in a light voice. "Out for fireflies, are you?"

"Yes," said Winnie.

"A lovely thing to do on a summer evening," said the man richly. "A lovely entertainment. I used to do it myself when I was your age. But of course that was a long, long time ago." He laughed, gesturing in self-deprecation with long, thin fingers. His tall body moved continuously; a foot tapped, a shoulder twitched. And it moved in angles, rather jerkily. But at the same time he had a kind of grace, like a well-handled marionette. Indeed, he seemed almost to hang suspended there in the twilight. But Winnie, though she was half charmed, was suddenly reminded of the stiff black ribbons they had hung on the door of the cottage for her grandfather's funeral. She frowned and looked at the man more closely. But his smile seemed perfectly all right, quite agreeable and friendly.

"Is this your house?" asked the man, folding his arms now and leaning against the gate.

"Yes," said Winnie. "Do you want to see my father?"

"Perhaps. In a bit," said the man. "But I'd like to talk to you first. Have you and your family lived here long?"

"Oh, yes," said Winnie. "We've lived here forever."

"Forever," the man echoed thoughtfully.

It was not a question, but Winnie decided to explain anyway. "Well, not forever, of course, but as long as there've been any people here. My grandmother was born here. She says this was all trees once, just one big forest everywhere around, but it's mostly all cut down now. Except for the wood."

"I see," said the man, pulling at his beard. "So of course you know everyone, and everything that goes on."

"Well, not especially," said Winnie. "At least, I don't. Why?"

The man lifted his eyebrows. "Oh," he said, "I'm looking for someone. A family."

"I don't know anybody much," said Winnie, with a shrug. "But my father might. You could ask him."

"I believe I shall," said the man. "I do believe I shall."

At this moment the cottage door opened, and in the lamp glow that spilled across the grass, Winnie's grandmother appeared. "Winifred? Who are you talking to out there?"

"It's a man, Granny," she called back. "He says he's looking for someone."

"What's that?" said the old woman. She picked up her skirts and came down the path to the gate. "What did you say he wants?"

The man on the other side of the fence bowed slightly. "Good evening, madam," he said. "How delightful to see you looking so fit."

"And why shouldn't I be fit?" she retorted, peering at him through the fading light. His yellow suit seemed to surprise her, and she squinted suspiciously. "We haven't met, that I can recall. Who are you? Who are you looking for?"

The man answered neither of these questions. Instead, he said, "This young lady tells me you've lived here for a long time, so I thought you would probably know everyone who comes and goes."

The old woman shook her head. "I *don't* know everyone," she said, "nor do I want to. And I don't stand outside in the dark discussing such a thing with strangers. Neither does Winifred. So . . ."

And then she paused. For, through the twilight sounds of crickets and sighing trees, a faint, surprising wisp of music came floating to them, and all three turned toward it, toward the wood. It was a tinkling little melody, and in a few moments it stopped.

"My stars!" said Winnie's grandmother, her eyes round. "I do believe it's come again, after all these years!" She pressed her wrinkled hands together, forgetting the man in the yellow suit. "Did you hear that, Winifred? That's it! That's the elf music I told you about. Why, it's been ages since I heard it last. And this is the first time you've *ever* heard it, isn't it? Wait till we tell your father!" And she seized Winnie's hand and turned to go back into the cottage.

"Wait!" said the man at the gate. He had stiffened, and his voice was eager. "You've heard that music before, you say?"

But, before he could get an answer, it began again and they all stopped to listen. This time it tinkled its way faintly through the little melody three times before it faded.

"It sounds like a music box," said Winnie when it was over.

"Nonsense. It's elves!" crowed her grandmother excitedly. And then she said to the man at the gate, "You'll have to excuse us now." She shook the gate latch under his nose, to make sure it was locked, and then, taking Winnie by the hand once more, she marched up the path into the cottage, shutting the door firmly behind her.

But the man in the yellow suit stood tapping his foot in the road for a long time all alone, looking at the wood. The last stains of sunset had melted away, and the twilight died, too, as he stood there, though its remnants clung reluctantly to everything that was pale in color—pebbles, the dusty road, the figure of the man himself—turning them blue and blurry.

Then the moon rose. The man came to himself and sighed. His expression was one of intense satisfaction. He put on his hat, and in the moonlight his long fingers were graceful and very white. Then he turned and disappeared down the shadowy road, and as he went he whistled, very softly, the tinkling little melody from the wood.

Chapter 5

WINNIE woke early the next morning. The sun was only just opening its own eye on the eastern horizon and the cottage was full of silence. But she realized that sometime during the night she had made up her mind: she would not run away today. "Where would I go, anyway?" she asked herself. "There's nowhere else I really want to be." But in another part of her head, the dark part where her oldest fears were housed, she knew there was another sort of reason for staying at home: she was afraid to go away alone.

It was one thing to talk about being by yourself, doing important things, but quite another when the opportunity arose. The characters in the stories she read always seemed to go off without a thought or care, but in real life—well, the world was a dangerous place. People were always telling her so. And she would not be able to manage without protection. They were always telling her that, too. No one ever said precisely what it was that she would not be able to manage. But she did not need to ask. Her own imagination supplied the horrors.

Still, it was galling, this having to admit she was afraid. And when she remembered the toad, she felt even more disheartened. What if the toad should be out by the fence again today?

What if he should laugh at her secretly and think she was a coward?

Well, anyway, she could at least slip out, right now, she decided, and go into the wood. To see if she could discover what had really made the music the night before. That would be something, anyway. She did not allow herself to consider the idea that making a difference in the world might require a bolder venture. She merely told herself consolingly, "Of course, while I'm in the wood, if I decide never to come back, well then, that will be that." She was able to believe in this because she needed to; and, believing, was her own true, promising friend once more.

It was another heavy morning, already hot and breathless, but in the wood the air was cooler and smelled agreeably damp. Winnie had been no more than two slow minutes walking timidly under the interlacing branches when she wondered why she had never come here before. "Why, it's nice!" she thought with great surprise.

For the wood was full of light, entirely different from the light she was used to. It was green and amber and alive, quivering in splotches on the padded ground, fanning into sturdy stripes between the tree trunks. There were little flowers she did not recognize, white and palest blue; and endless, tangled vines; and here and there a fallen log, half rotted but soft with patches of sweet green-velvet moss.

And there were creatures everywhere. The air fairly hummed with their daybreak activity: beetles and birds and squirrels and ants, and countless other things unseen, all gentle and self-absorbed and not in the least alarming. There was even, she saw with satisfaction, the toad. It was squatting on a low stump and she might not have noticed it, for it looked more like a mushroom than a living creature sitting there. As she came abreast of it, however, it blinked, and the movement gave it away.

"See?" she exclaimed. "I told you I'd be here first thing in the morning."

The toad blinked again and nodded. Or perhaps it was only swallowing a fly. But then it nudged itself off the edge of the stump and vanished in the underbrush.

"It must have been watching for me," said Winnie to herself, and was very glad she had come.

She wandered for a long time, looking at everything, listening to everything, proud to forget the tight, pruned world outside, humming a little now, trying to remember the pattern of the melody she had heard the night before. And then, up ahead, in a place where the light seemed brighter and the ground somewhat more open, something moved.

Winnie stopped abruptly and crouched down. "If it's really elves," she thought, "I can have a look at them." And, though her instinct was to turn and run, she was pleased to discover that her curiosity was stronger. She began to creep forward. She would go just close enough, she told herself. Just close enough to see. And *then* she would turn and run. But when she came near, up behind a sheltering tree trunk, and peered around it, her mouth dropped open and all thought of running melted away.

There was a clearing directly in front of her, at the center of which an enormous tree thrust up, its thick roots rumpling the ground ten feet around in every direction. Sitting relaxed with his back against the trunk was a boy, almost a man. And he seemed so glorious to Winnie that she lost her heart at once.

He was thin and sunburned, this wonderful boy, with a thick mop of curly brown hair, and he wore his battered trousers and loose, grubby shirt with as much self-assurance as if they were silk and satin. A pair of green suspenders, more decorative than useful, gave the finishing touch, for he was shoeless and there was a twig tucked between the toes of one foot. He waved the twig idly as he sat there, his face turned up to gaze at the branches far above him. The golden morning light seemed to glow all around him, while brighter patches fell, now on his lean, brown hands, now on his hair and face, as the leaves stirred over his head.

Then he rubbed an ear carelessly, yawned, and stretched. Shifting his position, he turned his attention to a little pile of pebbles next to him. As Winnie watched, scarcely breathing, he moved the pile carefully to one side, pebble by pebble. Beneath the pile, the ground was shiny wet. The boy lifted a final stone and Winnie saw a low spurt of water, arching up and returning, like a fountain, into the ground. He bent and put his lips to the spurt, drinking noiselessly, and then he sat up again and drew his shirt sleeve across his mouth. As he did this, he turned his face in her direction—and their eyes met.

For a long moment they looked at each other in silence, the boy with his arm still raised to his mouth. Neither of them moved. At last his arm fell to his side. "You may as well come out," he said, with a frown.

Winnie stood up, embarrassed and, because of that, resentful. "I didn't mean to watch you," she protested as she stepped into the clearing. "I didn't know anyone would be here."

The boy eyed her as she came forward. "What're *you* doing here?" he asked her sternly.

"It's my wood," said Winnie, surprised by the question. "I can come here whenever I want to. At least, I was never here before, but I *could* have come, any time."

"Oh," said the boy, relaxing a little. "You're one of the Fosters, then."

"I'm Winnie," she said. "Who are you?"

"I'm Jesse Tuck," he answered. "How do." And he put out a hand.

Winnie took his hand, staring at him. He was even more beautiful up close. "Do you live nearby?" she managed at last, letting go of his hand reluctantly. "I never saw you before. Do you come here a lot? No one's supposed to. It's our wood." Then she added quickly, "It's all right, though, if *you* come here. I mean, it's all right with *me*."

The boy grinned. "No, I don't live nearby, and no, I don't come here often. Just passing through. And thanks, I'm glad it's all right with you."

"That's good," said Winnie irrelevantly. She stepped back and sat down primly a short distance from him. "How old are you, anyway?" she asked, squinting at him.

There was a pause. At last he said, "Why do you want to know?"

"I just wondered," said Winnie.

"All right. I'm one hundred and four years old," he told her solemnly.

"No, I mean really," she persisted.

"Well then," he said, "if you must know, I'm seventeen."

"Seventeen?"

"That's right."

"Oh," said Winnie hopelessly. "Seventeen. That's old."

"You have no idea," he agreed with a nod.

Winnie had the feeling he was laughing at her, but decided it was a nice kind of laughing. "Are you married?" she asked next.

This time he laughed out loud. "No, I'm not married. Are you?"

Now it was Winnie's turn to laugh. "Of course not," she said. "I'm only ten. But I'll be eleven pretty soon."

"And *then* you'll get married," he suggested.

Winnie laughed again, her head on one side, admiring him. And then she pointed to the spurt of water. "Is that good to drink?" she asked. "I'm thirsty."

Jesse Tuck's face was instantly serious. "Oh, that. No—no, it's not," he said quickly. "You mustn't drink from it. Comes right up out of the ground. Probably pretty dirty." And he began to pile the pebbles over it again.

"But *you* drank some," Winnie reminded him.

"Oh. Did you see that?" He looked at her anxiously. "Well, me, I'll drink anything. I mean, I'm used to it. It wouldn't be good for *you*, though."

"Why not?" said Winnie. She stood up. "It's mine, anyway, if it's in the wood. I want some. I'm about dry as dust." And she went to where he sat, and knelt down beside the pile of pebbles.

"Believe me, Winnie Foster," said Jesse, "it would be terrible for you if you drank any of this water. Just terrible. I can't let you."

"Well, I still don't see why not," said Winnie plaintively. "I'm getting thirstier every minute. If it didn't hurt you, it won't hurt me. If my papa was here, he'd let me have some."

"You're not going to tell him about it, are you?" said Jesse. His face had gone very pale under its sunburn. He stood up and put a bare foot firmly on the pile of pebbles. "I knew this would happen sooner or later. *Now* what am I going to do?"

As he said this, there was a crashing sound among the trees and a voice called, "Jesse?"

"Thank goodness!" said Jesse, blowing out his cheeks in relief. "Here comes Ma and Miles. They'll know what to do."

And sure enough, a big, comfortable-looking woman appeared, leading a fat old horse, and at her side was a young man almost as beautiful as Jesse. It was Mae Tuck with her other son, Jesse's older brother. And at once, when she saw the two of them, Jesse with his foot on the pile of pebbles and Winnie on her knees beside him, she seemed to understand. Her hand flew to her bosom, grasping at the old brooch that fastened her shawl, and her face went bleak. "Well, boys," she said, "here it is. The worst is happening at last."

Chapter 6

AFTERWARD, when she thought about it, it seemed to Winnie that the next few minutes were only a blur. First she was kneeling on the ground, insisting on a drink from the spring, and the next thing she knew, she was seized and swung through the air, openmouthed, and found herself straddling the bouncing back of the fat old horse, with Miles and Jesse trotting along on either side, while Mae ran puffing ahead, dragging on the bridle.

Winnie had often been haunted by visions of what it would be like to be kidnapped. But none of her visions had been like this, with her kidnappers just as alarmed as she was herself. She had always pictured a troupe of burly men with long black moustaches who would tumble her into a blanket and bear her off like a sack of potatoes while she pleaded for mercy. But, instead, it was *they,* Mae Tuck and Miles and Jesse, who were pleading.

"Please, child . . . dear, dear child . . . don't you be scared." This was Mae, trying to run and call back over her shoulder at the same time. "We . . . wouldn't harm you . . . for the world."

"If you'd . . . yelled or anything"—this was Jesse—"someone might've heard you and . . . that's too risky."

And Miles said, "We'll explain it . . . soon as we're far enough away."

Winnie herself was speechless. She clung to the saddle and gave herself up to the astonishing fact that, though her heart was pounding and her backbone felt like a pipe full of cold running water, her head was fiercely calm. Disconnected thoughts presented themselves one by one, as if they had been waiting their turn in line. "So this is what it's like to ride a horse—I was going to run away today anyway—what will they say when I'm not there for breakfast—I wish the toad could see me now—that woman is worried about me—Miles is taller than Jesse—I'd better duck if I don't want this next branch to knock me off."

They had come to the edge of the wood now, with no sign of slowing their rapid jog. The road, where it angled across the meadow, was just ahead, dazzling white in the open sunlight. And there, standing on the road, was the man from the night before, the man in the yellow suit, his black hat on his head.

Discovering him, seeing his surprise, and presented at once with choices, Winnie's mind perversely went blank. Instead of crying out for help, she merely goggled at him as they fled past the spot where he stood. Mae Tuck was the only one who spoke, and the most she could offer was: "Teaching our little girl . . . how to ride!" Only then did it come to Winnie that she ought to shout, wave her arms, do *something.* But the man had fallen away behind by that time, and she was afraid to let go of the saddle, afraid to turn around, lest she fall off the horse. In another moment it was too late. They had sped up the hill and down its other side, and the opportunity was lost.

After another few minutes, the road led them to a place where, off to the left, a shallow stream looped near, with willows and sheltering, scrubby bushes. "Stop!" cried Mae. "We'll stop here!" Miles and Jesse grabbed at the horse's harness and he pulled up abruptly, nearly toppling Winnie off over his neck. "Lift the poor child down," Mae gasped, her chest heaving. "We'll go catch our breath by the water and try to put things straight before we go on."

But the explanation, once they had stumbled to the banks of the stream, came hard. Mae seemed embarrassed, and Miles and Jesse fidgeted, glancing at their mother uneasily. No one knew how to begin. For her part, Winnie, now that the running was over, began to comprehend what was happening, and with the comprehension her throat closed and her mouth went dry as paper. This was no vision. This was real. Strangers were taking her away; they might do anything; she might never see her mother again. And then, thinking of her mother, she saw herself as small, weak, and helpless, and she began to cry, suddenly, crushed as much by outrage as by shock.

Mae Tuck's round face wrinkled in dismay. "Dear Lord, don't cry! Please don't cry, child!" she implored. "We're not bad people, truly we're not. We *had* to bring you away—you'll see why in a minute—and we'll take you back just as soon as we can. Tomorrow. I promise."

When Mae said, "Tomorrow," Winnie's sobs turned to wails. Tomorrow! It was like being told she would be kept away forever. She wanted to go home now, at once, rush back to the safety of the fence and her mother's voice from the window. Mae reached out to her, but she twisted away, her hands over her face, and gave herself up to weeping.

"This is awful!" said Jesse. "Can't you do something, Ma? The poor little tad."

"We ought to've had some better plan than *this*," said Miles.

"That's the truth," said Mae helplessly. "The dear Lord knows there's been time enough to think of one, and it had to happen sooner or later. We been plain bone lucky it hasn't before now. But I never expected it'd be a *child!*" She reached distractedly into the pocket of her skirt and took out the music box and, without thinking, twisted the winding key with trembling fingers.

When the tinkling little melody began, Winnie's sobbing slowed. She stood by the stream, her hands still over her face, and listened. Yes, it was the same music she had heard the night before. Somehow it calmed her. It was like a ribbon tying her to familiar things. She thought, "When I get home, I'll tell Granny it wasn't elf music after all." She wiped her face as well as she could with her wet hands and turned to Mae. "That's the music I heard last night," she managed between recovering

17

snuffles. "When I was out in my yard. My granny said it was elves."

"Dear me, no," said Mae, peering at her hopefully. "It's only my music box. I didn't suppose anyone could hear it." She held it out to Winnie. "Do you want to take a look at it?"

"It's pretty," said Winnie, taking the little box and turning it over in her hands. The winding key was still revolving, but more and more slowly. The melody faltered. Another few widely spaced notes plinked, and then it stopped.

"Wind it up if you want to," said Mae. "Clockwise."

Winnie turned the key. It clicked faintly. And then, after several more turns, the music began to play again, brisk from its fresh winding, and merry. No one who owned a thing like this could be too disagreeable. Winnie examined the painted roses and lilies of the valley, and smiled in spite of herself. "It's pretty," she repeated, handing it back to Mae.

The music box had relaxed them all. Miles dragged a handkerchief from a back pocket and mopped at his face, and Mae sank down heavily on a rock, pulling off the blue straw hat and fanning herself with it.

"Look here, Winnie Foster," said Jesse. "We're friends, we really are. But you got to help us. Come sit down, and we'll try to tell you why."

Chapter 7

IT was the strangest story Winnie had ever heard. She soon suspected they had never told it before, except to each other—that she was their first real audience; for they gathered around her like children at their mother's knee, each trying to claim her attention, and sometimes they all talked at once, and interrupted each other, in their eagerness.

Eighty-seven years before, the Tucks had come from a long way to the east, looking for a place to settle. In those days the wood was not a wood, it was a forest, just as her grandmother had said: a forest that went on and on and on. They had thought they would start a farm, as soon as they came to the end of the trees. But the trees never seemed to end. When they came to the part that was now the wood, and turned from the trail to find a camping place, they happened on the spring. "It was real nice," said Jesse with a sigh. "It looked just the way it does now. A clearing, lots of sunshine, that big tree with all those knobby roots. We stopped and everyone took a drink, even the horse."

"No," said Mae, "the cat didn't drink. That's important."

"Yes," said Miles, "don't leave that out. We all had a drink, except for the cat."

"Well, anyway," Jesse went on, "the water tasted—sort of strange. But we camped there overnight. And Pa carved a T on the tree trunk, to mark where we'd been. And then we went on."

They had come out of the forest at last, many miles to the west, had found a thinly populated valley, had started their farm. "We put up a house for Ma and Pa," said Miles, "and a little shack for Jesse and me. We figured *we'd* be starting families of our own pretty soon and would want our own houses."

"That was the first time we figured there was something peculiar," said Mae. "Jesse fell out of a tree . . ."

"I was way up in the middle," Jesse interrupted, "trying to saw off some of the big branches before we cut her down. I lost my balance and I fell . . ."

"He landed plum on his head," said Mae with a shudder. "We thought for sure he'd broke his neck. But come to find out, it didn't hurt him a bit!"

"Not long after," Miles went on, "some hunters come by one day at sunset. The horse was out grazing by some trees and they shot him. Mistook him for a deer, they said. Can you fancy that? But the thing is, they didn't kill him. The bullet went right on through him, and didn't hardly even leave a mark."

"Then Pa got snake bite . . ."

"And Jesse ate the poison toadstools . . ."

"And I cut myself," said Mae. "Remember? Slicing bread."

But it was the passage of time that worried them most. They had worked the farm, settled down, made friends. But after ten years, then twenty, they had to face the fact that there was something terribly wrong. None of them was getting any older.

"I was more'n forty by then," said Miles sadly. "I was married. I had two children. But, from the look of me, I was still twenty-two. My wife, she finally made up her mind I'd sold my soul to the Devil. She left me. She went away and she took the children with her."

"I'm glad *I* never got married," Jesse put in.

"It was the same with our friends," said Mae. "They come to pull back from us. There was talk about witchcraft. Black magic. Well, you can't hardly blame them, but finally we had to leave the farm. We didn't know where to go. We started back the way we come, just wandering. We was like gypsies. When we got this far, it'd changed, of course. A lot of the trees was gone. There was people, and Treegap—it was a new village. The road was here, but in those days it was mostly just a cow path. We went on into what was left of the wood to make a camp, and when we got to the clearing and the tree and the spring, we remembered it from before."

"*It* hadn't changed, no more'n we had," said Miles. "And that was how we found out. Pa'd carved a T on the tree, remember, twenty years before, but the T was just where it'd been when he done it. That tree hadn't grown one whit in all that time. It was exactly the same. And the T he'd carved was as fresh as if it'd just been put there."

Then they had remembered drinking the water. They—and the horse. But not the cat. The cat had lived a long and happy life on the farm, but had died some ten years before. So they decided at last that the source of their changelessness was the spring.

"When we come to that conclusion," Mae went on, "Tuck said—that's my husband, Angus Tuck—he said he had to be sure, once and for all. He took his shotgun and he pointed it at hisself the best way he could, and before we could stop him, he pulled the trigger." There was a long pause. Mae's fingers, laced together in her lap, twisted with the tension of remembering. At last she said, "The shot knocked him down. Went into his heart. It *had* to, the way he aimed. And right on through him. It scarcely even left a mark. Just like—*you* know—like you shot a bullet through water. And he was just the same as if he'd never done it."

"After that we went sort of crazy," said Jesse, grinning at the memory. "Heck, we was going to live forever. Can you picture what it felt like to find that out?"

"But then we sat down and talked it over . . ." said Miles.

"We're still talking it over," Jesse added.

"And we figured it'd be very bad if everyone knowed about that spring," said Mae. "We begun to see what it would mean." She peered at Winnie. "Do you understand, child? That water—it stops you right where you are. If you'd had a drink of it today, you'd stay a little girl forever. You'd never grow up, not ever."

"We don't know how it works, or even why," said Miles.

"Pa thinks it's something left over from—well, from some other plan for the way the world should be," said Jesse. "Some plan that didn't work out too good. And so everything was changed. Except that the spring was passed over, somehow or other. Maybe he's right. *I* don't know. But you see, Winnie Foster, when

I told you before I'm a hundred and four years old, I was telling the truth. But I'm really only seventeen. And, so far as I know, I'll stay seventeen till the end of the world."

Chapter 8

WINNIE did not believe in fairy tales. She had never longed for a magic wand, did not expect to marry a prince, and was scornful—most of the time—of her grandmother's elves. So now she sat, mouth open, wide-eyed, not knowing what to make of this extraordinary story. It couldn't—not a bit of it—be true. And yet:

"It feels so fine to tell somebody!" Jesse exploded. "Just think, Winnie Foster, you're the only person in the world, besides us, who knows about it!"

"Hold on now," said Miles cautiously. "Maybe not. There might be a whole lot of others, for all we know, wandering around just like us."

"Maybe. But *we* don't know them," Jesse pointed out. "We've never had anyone but us to talk about it to. Winnie—isn't it peculiar? And kind of wonderful? Just think of all the things we've seen in the world! All the things we're going to see!"

"That kind of talk'll make her want to rush back and drink a gallon of the stuff," warned Miles. "There's a whole lot more to it than Jesse Tuck's good times, you know."

"Oh, stuff," said Jesse with a shrug. "We might as well enjoy it, long as we can't change it. You don't have to be such a parson all the time."

"I'm not being a parson," said Miles. "I just think you ought to take it more serious."

"Now, boys," said Mae. She was kneeling by the stream, splashing her face and hands with cool water. "Whew! Such weather!" she exclaimed, sitting back on her heels. She unfastened the brooch, took off her shawl, and toweled her dripping face. "Well, child," she said to Winnie, standing up, "now you share our secret. It's a big, dangerous secret. We got to have your help to keep it. I expect you're full of questions, but we can't stay here no longer." She tied the shawl around her waist then, and sighed. "It pains me to think how your ma and pa will worry, but there's just no way around it. We got to take you home with us. That's the plan. Tuck—he'll want to talk it out, make sure you see why you can't tell no one. But we'll bring you back tomorrow. All right?" And all three of them looked at her hopefully.

"All right," said Winnie. For, she decided, there wasn't any choice. She would have to go. They would probably make her go, anyway, no matter what she said. But she felt there was nothing to be afraid of, not really. For they seemed gentle. Gentle and—in a strange way—childlike. They made her feel old. And the way they spoke to her, the way they looked at her, made her feel special. Important. It was a warm, spreading feeling, entirely new. She liked it, and in spite of their story, she liked them, too—especially Jesse.

But it was Miles who took her hand and said, "It's really fine to have you along, even if it's only for a day or two."

Then Jesse gave a great whoop and leapt into the stream, splashing mightily. "What'd you bring for breakfast, Ma?" he cried. "We can eat on the way, can't we? I'm starving!"

So, with the sun riding high now in the sky, they started off again, noisy in the August stillness, eating bread and cheese. Jesse sang funny old songs in a loud voice and swung like a monkey from the branches of trees, showing off shamelessly for Winnie, calling to her, "Hey, Winnie Foster, watch me!" and "Look what I can do!"

And Winnie, laughing at him, lost the last of her alarm. They were friends, *her* friends. She was running away after all, but she was not alone. Closing the gate on her oldest fears as she had closed the gate of her own fenced yard, she discovered the wings she'd always wished she had. And all at once she was elated. Where were the terrors she'd been told she should expect? She could not recognize them anywhere. The sweet earth opened out its wide four corners to her like the petals of a flower ready to be picked, and it shimmered with light and possibility till she was dizzy with it. Her mother's voice, the feel of home, receded for the moment, and her thoughts turned forward. Why, she, too, might live forever in this remarkable world she was only just discovering! The story of the spring—it might be true! So that, when she was not rolling along on the back of the fat old horse—by choice, this time—she ran shouting down the road, her arms flung out, making more noise than anybody.

It was good. So good, in fact, that through it all, not one of them noticed that the man they had passed on the road, the man in the yellow suit, had crept up to the bushes by the stream and heard it all, the whole fantastic story. Nor did they notice that he was following now, beside the road far behind, his mouth, above the thin, gray beard, turned ever so slightly toward a smile.

Chapter 9

THE August sun rolled up, hung at mid-heaven for a blinding hour, and at last wheeled westward before the journey was done. But Winnie was exhausted long before that. Miles carried her some of the way. The tops of her cheeks were bright pink with sunburn, her nose a vivid, comic red, but she had been rescued from a more serious broiling by Mae, who had finally insisted that she wear the blue straw hat. It came down far over her ears and gave her a clownish appearance, but the shade from its brim was so welcome that Winnie put vanity aside and dozed gratefully in Miles's strong arms, her own arms wound around his neck.

The pastures, fields, and scrubby groves they crossed were vigorous with bees, and crickets leapt before them as if each step released a spring and flung them up like pebbles. But everything else was motionless, dry as biscuit, on the brink of burning, hoarding final reservoirs of sap, trying to hold out till the rain returned, and Queen Anne's lace lay dusty on the surface of the meadows like foam on a painted sea.

It was amazing, then, to climb a long hill, to see ahead another hill, and beyond that the deep green of a scattered pine forest, and as you climbed, to feel the air ease and soften. Winnie revived, sniffing, and was able to ride the horse again, perched behind Mae. And to her oft-repeated question, "Are we almost there?" the welcome answer came at last: "Only a few more minutes now."

A wide stand of dark pines rose up, loomed nearer, and suddenly Jesse was crying, "We're home! This is it, Winnie Foster!" And he and Miles raced on and disappeared among the trees. The horse followed, turning onto a rutted path lumpy with roots, and it was as if they had slipped in under a giant colander. The late sun's brilliance could penetrate only in scattered glimmers, and everything was silent and untouched, the ground muffled with moss and sliding needles, the graceful arms of the pines stretched out protectively in every direction. And it was cool, blessedly cool and green. The horse picked his way carefully, and then ahead the path dropped down a steep embankment; and beyond that, Winnie, peering around Mae's bulk, saw a flash of color and a dazzling sparkle. Down the embankment they swayed and there it was, a plain, homely little house, barn-red, and below it the last of the sun flashing on the wrinkled surface of a tiny lake.

"Oh, *look!*" cried Winnie. "Water!"

At the same time, they heard two enormous splashes, two voices roaring with pleasure.

"It don't take 'em more'n a minute to pile into that pond," said Mae, beaming. "Well, you can't blame 'em in heat like this. You can go in, too, if you want."

Then they were at the door of the little house and Tuck was standing there. "Where's the child?" he demanded, for Winnie was hidden behind his wife. "The boys say you brung along a real, honest-to-goodness, natural child!"

"So I did," said Mae, sliding down off the horse, "and here she is."

Winnie's shyness returned at once when she saw the big man with his sad face and baggy trousers, but as he gazed at her, the warm, pleasing feeling spread through her again. For Tuck's head tilted to one side, his eyes went soft, and the gentlest smile in the world displaced the melancholy creases of his cheeks. He reached up to lift her from the horse's back and he said, "There's just no words to tell you how happy I am to see you. It's the finest thing that's happened in . . ." He interrupted himself, setting Winnie on the ground, and turned to Mae. "Does she know?"

"Course she knows," said Mae. "That's why I brung her back. Winnie, here's my husband, Angus Tuck. Tuck, meet Winnie Foster."

"How do, Winnie Foster," said Tuck, shaking Winnie's hand rather solemnly. "Well, then!" He straightened and peered down at her, and Winnie, looking back into his face, saw an expression there that made her feel like an unexpected present, wrapped in pretty paper and tied with ribbons, in spite of Mae's blue hat, which still enveloped her head. "Well, then," Tuck repeated, "seeing you know, I'll go on and say this is the finest thing that's happened in—oh—at least eighty years."

Chapter 10

WINNIE had grown up with order. She was used to it. Under the pitiless double assaults of her mother and grandmother, the cottage where she lived was always squeaking clean, mopped and swept and scoured into limp submission. There was no room for carelessness, no putting things off until later. The Foster women had made a fortress out of duty. Within it, they were indomitable. And Winnie was in training.

So she was unprepared for the homely little house beside the pond, unprepared for the gentle eddies of dust, the silver cobwebs, the mouse who lived—and welcome to him!—in a table drawer. There were only three rooms. The kitchen came first, with an open cabinet where dishes were stacked in perilous towers without the least regard for their varying dimensions. There was an enormous black stove, and a metal sink, and every surface, every wall, was piled and strewn and hung with everything imaginable, from onions to lanterns to wooden spoons to washtubs. And in a corner stood Tuck's forgotten shotgun.

The parlor came next, where the furniture, loose and sloping with age, was set about helter-skelter. An ancient green-plush sofa lolled alone in the center, like yet another mossy fallen log, facing a soot-streaked fireplace still deep in last winter's ashes. The table with the drawer that housed the mouse was pushed off, also alone, into a far corner, and three armchairs and an elderly rocker stood about aimlessly, like strangers at a party, ignoring each other.

Beyond this was the bedroom, where a vast and tipsy brass bed took up most of the space, but there was room beside it for the washstand with the lonely mirror, and opposite its foot a cavernous oak wardrobe from which leaked the faint smell of camphor.

Up a steep flight of narrow stairs was a dusty loft—"That's where the boys sleep when they're home," Mae explained—and that was all. And yet it was not quite all. For there was everywhere evidence of their activities, Mae's and Tuck's. Her sewing: patches and scraps of bright cloth; half-completed quilts and braided rugs; a bag of cotton batting with wisps of its contents, like snow, drifting into cracks and corners; the arms of the sofa webbed with strands of thread and dangerous with needles. His wood carving: curly shavings furring the floor, and little heaps of splinters and chips; every surface dim with the sawdust of countless sandings; limbs of unassembled dolls and wooden soldiers; a ship model propped on the mouse's table, waiting for its glue to dry; and a stack of wooden bowls, their sides smoothed to velvet, the topmost bowl filled with a jumble of big wooden spoons and forks, like dry, bleached bones. "We make things to sell," said Mae, surveying the mess approvingly.

And still this was not all. For, on the old beamed ceiling of the parlor, streaks of light swam and danced and wavered like a bright mirage, reflected through the windows from the sunlit surface of the pond. There were bowls of daisies everywhere, gay white and yellow. And over everything was the clean, sweet smell of the water and its weeds, the chatter of a swooping kingfisher, the carol and trill of a dozen other kinds of bird, and occasionally the thrilling bass note of an unastonished bullfrog at ease somewhere along the muddy banks.

Into it all came Winnie, eyes wide, and very much amazed. It was a whole new idea to her that people could live in such disarray, but at the same time she was charmed. It was . . . comfortable. Climbing behind Mae up the stairs to see the loft, she thought to herself: "Maybe it's because they think they have forever to clean it up." And this was followed by another thought, far more revolutionary: "Maybe they just don't care!"

"The boys don't be home very much," said Mae as they came up into the half light of the loft. "But when they are, they bed up here. There's plenty of room." The loft was cluttered, too, with all kinds of odds and ends, but there were two mattresses rolled out on the floor, and fresh sheets and blankets were folded almost neatly on each, waiting to be spread.

"Where do they go when they're away?" asked Winnie. "What do they do?"

"Oh," said Mae, "they go different places, do different things. They work at what jobs they can get, try to bring home some of their money. Miles can do carpentering, and he's a pretty fair blacksmith, too. Jesse now, *he* don't ever seem too settled in himself. Course, he's young." She stopped and smiled. "That sounds funny, don't it? Still, it's true, just the same. So Jesse, he does what strikes him at the moment, working in the fields, or in saloons, things like that, whatever he comes across. But they can't stay on in any one place for long, you know. None of us can. People get to wondering." She sighed. "We been in this house about as long as we dare, going on twenty years. It's a right nice place. Tuck's got so's he's real attached to it. Then, too, it's off by itself, plenty of fish in the pond, not too far from the towns around. When we need things, we go sometimes to one, sometimes the next, so people don't come to notice us much. And we sell where we can. But I guess we'll be moving on, one of these days. It's just about time."

It sounded rather sad to Winnie, never to belong anywhere. "That's too bad," she said, glancing shyly at Mae. "Always moving around and never having any friends or anything."

But Mae shrugged off this observation. "Tuck and me, we got each other," she said, "and that's a lot. The boys, now, they go their separate ways. They're some different, don't always get on too good. But they come home whenever the spirit moves, and every ten years, first week of August, they meet at the spring and come home *together* so's we can be a family again for a little while. That's why we was there this morning. One way or another, it all works out." She folded her arms and nodded, more to herself than to Winnie. "Life's got to be lived, no matter how long or short," she said calmly. "You got to take what comes. We just go along, like everybody else, one day at a time. Funny—we don't feel no different. Leastways, I don't. Sometimes I forget about what's happened to us, forget it altogether. And then sometimes it comes over me and I wonder why it happened to *us*. We're plain as salt, us Tucks. We don't deserve no blessings—if it is a blessing. And, likewise, I don't see how we deserve to be cursed, if it's a curse. Still—there's no use trying to figure why things fall the way they do. Things just are, and fussing don't bring changes. Tuck, now, he's got a few other ideas, but I expect he'll tell you. There! The boys are in from the pond."

Winnie heard a burst of voices downstairs, and in a moment Miles and Jesse were climbing to the loft.

"Here, child," said Mae hastily. "Hide your eyes. Boys? Are you decent? What'd you put on to swim in? I got Winnie up here, do you hear me?"

"For goodness' sake, Ma," said Jesse, emerging from the stairwell. "You think we're going to march around in our altogether with Winnie Foster in the house?"

And Miles, behind him, said, "We just jumped in with our clothes on. Too hot and tired to shed 'em."

It was true. They stood there side by side with their wet clothes plastered to their skins, little pools of water collecting at their feet.

"Well!" said Mae, relieved. "All right. Find something dry to put on. Your pa's got supper nearly ready." And she hustled Winnie down the narrow stairs.

Chapter 11

IT was a good supper, flapjacks, bacon, bread, and applesauce, but they ate sitting about in the parlor instead of around a table. Winnie had never had a meal that way before and she watched them carefully at first, to see what rules there might be that she did not know about. But there seemed to be no rules. Jesse sat on the floor and used the seat of a chair for a table, but the others held their plates in their laps. There were no napkins. It was all right, then, to lick the maple syrup from your fingers. Winnie was never allowed to do such a thing at home, but she had always thought it would be the easiest way. And suddenly the meal seemed luxurious.

After a few minutes, however, it was clear to Winnie that there was at least one rule: As long as there was food to eat, there was no conversation. All four Tucks kept their eyes and their attention on the business at hand. And in the silence, given time to think, Winnie felt her elation, and her thoughtless pleasure, wobble and collapse.

It had been different when they were out-of-doors, where the world belonged to everyone and no one. Here, everything was theirs alone, everything was done their way. Eating, she realized now, was a very personal thing, not something to do with strangers. *Chewing* was a personal thing. Yet here she was, chewing with strangers in a strange place. She shivered a little, and frowned, looking round at them. That story they had told her—why, they were crazy, she thought harshly, and they were criminals. They had kidnapped her, right out of the middle of her very own wood, and now she would be expected to sleep—*all night*—in this dirty, peculiar house. She had never slept in any bed but her own in her life. All these thoughts flowed at once from the dark part of her mind. She put down her fork and said, unsteadily, "I want to go home."

The Tucks stopped eating, and looked at her, surprised. Mae said soothingly, "Why, of course you do, child. That's only nat-ural. I'll take you home. I promised I would, soon's we've ex-plained a bit as to why you got to promise you'll never tell about the spring. That's the only reason we brung you here. We got to make you see why."

Then Miles said, cheerfully and with sudden sympathy, "There's a pretty good old rowboat. I'll take you out for a row after supper."

"No, *I* will," said Jesse. "Let *me*. I found her first, didn't I, Win-nie Foster? Listen, I'll show you where the frogs are, and . . ."

"Hush," Tuck interrupted. "Everyone hush. *I'll* take Winnie rowing on the pond. There's a good deal to be said and I think we better hurry up and say it. I got a feeling there ain't a whole lot of time."

Jesse laughed at this, and ran a hand roughly through his curls. "That's funny, Pa. Seems to me like time's the only thing we got a lot of."

But Mae frowned. "You worried, Tuck? What's got you? No one saw us on the way up. Well, now, wait a bit—yes, they did, come to think of it. There was a man on the road, just outside Treegap. But he didn't say nothing."

"He knows me, though," said Winnie. She had forgotten, too, about the man in the yellow suit, and now, thinking of him, she felt a surge of relief. "He'll tell my father he saw me."

"He knows you?" said Mae, her frown deepening. "But you didn't call out to him, child. Why not?"

"I was too scared to do *anything*," said Winnie honestly.

Tuck shook his head. "I never thought we'd come to the place where we'd be scaring children," he said. "I guess there's no way to make it up to you, Winnie, but I'm sure most awful sorry it had to happen like that. Who was this man you saw?"

"I don't know his name," said Winnie. "But he's a pretty nice man, I guess." In fact, he seemed supremely nice to her now, a kind of savior. And then she added, "He came to our house last night, but he didn't go inside."

"Well, that don't sound too serious, Pa," said Miles. "Just some stranger passing by."

"Just the same, we got to get you home again, Winnie," said Tuck, standing up decisively. "We got to get you home just as fast as we can. I got a feeling this whole thing is going to come apart like wet bread. But first we got to talk, and the pond's the best place. The pond's got answers. Come along, child. Let's go out on the water."

Chapter 12

THE sky was a ragged blaze of red and pink and orange, and its double trembled on the surface of the pond like color spilled from a paintbox. The sun was dropping fast now, a soft red sliding egg yolk, and already to the east there was a darkening to purple. Winnie, newly brave with her thoughts of being rescued, climbed boldly into the rowboat. The hard heels of her buttoned boots made a hollow banging sound against its wet boards, loud in the warm and breathless quiet. Across the pond a bullfrog spoke a deep note of warning. Tuck climbed in, too, pushing off, and, settling the oars into their locks, dipped them into the silty bottom in one strong pull. The rowboat slipped from the bank then, silently, and glided out, tall water grasses whispering away from its sides, releasing it.

Here and there the still surface of the water dimpled, and bright rings spread noiselessly and vanished. "Feeding time," said Tuck softly. And Winnie, looking down, saw hosts of tiny insects skittering and skating on the surface. "Best time of all for fishing," he said, "when they come up to feed."

He dragged on the oars. The rowboat slowed and began to drift gently toward the farthest end of the pond. It was so quiet that Winnie almost jumped when the bullfrog spoke again. And then, from the tall pines and birches that ringed the pond, a wood thrush caroled. The silver notes were pure and clear and lovely.

"Know what that is, all around us, Winnie?" said Tuck, his voice low. "Life. Moving, growing, changing, never the same two minutes together. This water, you look out at it every morning, and it *looks* the same, but it ain't. All night long it's been moving, coming in through the stream back there to the west, slipping out through the stream down east here, always quiet, always new, moving on. You can't hardly see the current, can you? And sometimes the wind makes it look like it's going the other way. But it's always there, the water's always moving on, and someday, after a long while, it comes to the ocean."

They drifted in silence for a time. The bullfrog spoke again, and from behind them, far back in some reedy, secret place, another bullfrog answered. In the fading light, the trees along the banks were slowly losing their dimensions, flattening into silhouettes clipped from black paper and pasted to the paling sky. The voice of a different frog, hoarser and not so deep, croaked from the nearest bank.

"Know what happens then?" said Tuck. "To the water? The sun sucks some of it up right out of the ocean and carries it back in clouds, and then it rains, and the rain falls into the stream, and the stream keeps moving on, taking it all back again. It's a wheel, Winnie. Everything's a wheel, turning and turning, never stopping. The frogs is part of it, and the bugs, and the fish, and the wood thrush, too. And people. But never the same ones. Always coming in new, always growing and changing, and always moving on. That's the way it's supposed to be. That's the way it *is*."

The rowboat had drifted at last to the end of the pond, but now its bow bumped into the rotting branches of a fallen tree that thrust thick fingers into the water. And though the current pulled at it, dragging its stern sidewise, the boat was wedged and could not follow. The water slipped past it, out between clumps of reeds and brambles, and gurgled down a narrow bed, over stones and pebbles, foaming a little, moving swiftly now after its slow trip between the pond's wide banks. And, farther down, Winnie could see that it hurried into a curve, around a leaning willow, and disappeared.

"It goes on," Tuck repeated, "to the ocean. But this rowboat now, it's stuck. If we didn't move it out ourself, it would stay here forever, trying to get loose, but stuck. That's what us Tucks are, Winnie. Stuck so's we can't move on. We ain't part of the wheel no more. Dropped off, Winnie. Left behind. And everywhere around us, things is moving and growing and changing. You, for instance. A child now, but someday a woman. And after that, moving on to make room for the new children."

Winnie blinked, and all at once her mind was drowned with understanding of what he was saying. For she—yes, even she—would go out of the world willy-nilly someday. Just go out, like the flame of a candle, and no use protesting. It was a certainty. She would try very hard not to think of it, but sometimes, as now, it would be forced upon her. She raged against it, helpless and insulted, and blurted at last, "I don't want to die."

"No," said Tuck calmly. "Not now. Your time's not now. But dying's part of the wheel, right there next to being born. You can't pick out the pieces you like and leave the rest. Being part of the whole thing, that's the blessing. But it's passing us by, us Tucks. Living's heavy work, but off to one side, the way *we* are, it's useless, too. It don't make sense. If I knowed how to climb back on the wheel, I'd do it in a minute. You can't have living without dying. So you can't call it living, what we got. We just *are*, we just *be*, like rocks beside the road."

Tuck's voice was rough now, and Winnie, amazed, sat rigid. No one had ever talked to her of things like this before. "I want to grow again," he said fiercely, "and change. And if that means I got to move on at the end of it, then I want that, too. Listen, Winnie, it's something you don't find out how you feel until afterwards. If people knowed about the spring down there in Tree-gap, they'd all come running like pigs to slops. They'd trample each other, trying to get some of that water. That'd be bad enough, but afterwards—can you imagine? All the little ones little forever, all the old ones old forever. Can you picture what that means? *Forever?* The wheel would keep on going round, the water rolling by to the ocean, but the people would've turned into nothing but rocks by the side of the road. 'Cause they wouldn't know till after, and then it'd be too late." He peered at her, and Winnie saw that his face was pinched with the effort of explaining. "Do you see, now, child? Do you understand? Oh, Lord, I just got to make you understand!"

There was a long, long moment of silence. Winnie, struggling with the anguish of all these things, could only sit hunched and numb, the sound of the water rolling in her ears. It was black and silky now; it lapped at the sides of the rowboat and hurried on around them into the stream.

And then, down the length of the pond, a voice rang out. It was Miles, and every word, across the water, came clearly to their ears. "Pa! Pa, come back! Something's happened, Pa. The horse is gone. Can you hear me? Someone's stole the horse."

Chapter 13

SOMETIME later, the man in the yellow suit slipped down from the saddle and tied the Tucks' old horse to a bar of the Fosters' fence. He tried the gate. It was unlocked. He pushed through and strode up the path to the door of the cottage. Though it was very late now, almost midnight, the windows glowed golden: the family had not gone to bed. The man in the yellow suit took off his hat and smoothed his hair with long white fingers. Then he knocked at the door. It was opened at once by Winnie's grandmother, and before she could speak, the man said quickly, "Ah! Good evening! May I come in? I have happy news for you. I know where they've taken the little girl."

Chapter 14

THERE had been nothing for the Tucks to do but go to bed. It was too dark now to go out looking for the horse thief, and anyway, they had no idea when he had done his thieving or which way he had gone.

"That beats all, though, don't it, Pa," said Jesse, "coming up to a person's house and stealing their horse right out from under their nose!"

"I got to give you that," said Tuck. "But the question is, was it just some ordinary thief, or was it someone that had some special reason? I don't like it. I got a bad feeling about the whole thing."

"Hush now, Tuck," said Mae. She was spreading a quilt on the old sofa, making it into a bed for Winnie. "You're too much of a worrier. There's nothing we can do about it now, so there's no sense fussing. You got no reason to think there's anything peculiar about it, anyway. Come on, we'll get a good night's sleep and figure it out in the morning when we're fresh. Boys, up you go, and don't get talking—you'll keep us awake. Winnie, child, you bed down, too. You'll sleep first-rate on the sofa here."

But Winnie did not sleep at all, not for a long, long time. The cushions of the sofa were remarkably lumpy and smelled like old newspapers; and the chair pad Mae had given her for a pillow was thin and hard, and rough under her cheek. But far worse than this was the fact that she was still in her clothes, for she had firmly refused the offer of Mae's spare nightgown, with its seeming miles of faded cotton flannel. Only her own night-gown would do, and the regular bedtime routine; without them, she was painfully lonely for home. Her joy on the road that morning had completely disappeared; the wide world shrank and her oldest fears rolled freely in her consciousness. It was unbelievable that she should be in this place; it was an outrage. But she was helpless to do anything about it, helpless to control it, and exhausted by the conversation in the rowboat.

Was it true? Could they really never die, these Tucks? It had evidently not occurred to them that she might not believe it. They were only concerned that she keep the secret. Well, she did not believe it. It was nonsense. Wasn't it? Well, wasn't it?

Winnie's head whirled. Remembering the man in the yellow suit was the only thing that kept her from weeping. "He's told them by now," she thought, rehearsing it. "They've been looking for me for hours. But they don't know where to look! No. The man saw which way we were headed. Papa will find me. They're out looking for me right now."

She went over it again and again, lying wrapped in the quilt, while outside the moon rose, turning the pond to silver. There was a hint of mist, now that the air was cooler, and the frogs talked comfortably. Crickets soon joined in with their shrill, rhythmic song. In the table drawer, the mouse rustled softly, enjoying the supper of flapjack crumbs Mae had put there for him. And at last these things were clearer in Winnie's ears than the voice of her thoughts. She began to relax, listening to the sound-filled silence. Then, just as she was drifting into sleep, she heard soft footsteps and Mae was beside her. "You resting easy, child?" she whispered.

"I'm all right, thank you," said Winnie.

"I'm sorry about everything," said Mae. "I just didn't know no other way but to bring you back with us. I know it ain't very happy for you here, but . . . well . . . anyway, you have a good talk with Tuck?"

"I guess so," said Winnie.

"That's good. Well. I'm going back to bed. Get a good sleep."

"All right," said Winnie.

But still Mae lingered. "We been alone so long," she said at last, "I guess we don't know how to do with visitors. But still and all, it's a good feeling, you being here with us. I wish you was . . . ours." She put out an awkward hand then and touched Winnie's hair. "Well," she said, "good night."

"Good night," said Winnie.

Tuck came, too, a little later, to peer down at her anxiously. He was wearing a long white nightshirt and his hair was rumpled. "Oh!" he said. "You still awake? Everything all right?"

"Yes," said Winnie.

"I didn't mean to go disturbing you," he said. "But I been laying in there thinking I ought to be setting out here with you till you went to sleep."

"You don't have to do that," said Winnie, surprised and touched. "I'm all right."

He looked uncertain. "Well . . . but if you want something, will you holler? I'm just in the next room—I'd be out here like a shot." And then he added, gruffly, "It's been quite a time since we had a natural, growing child in the house . . ." His voice trailed off. "Well. Try to get some sleep. That sofa there, I guess it ain't the kind of thing you're used to."

"It's fine," said Winnie.

"The bed's no better, or I'd switch with you," he said. He didn't seem to know how to finish the conversation. But then he bent and kissed her quickly on the cheek, and was gone.

Winnie lay with her eyes wide. She felt cared for and—confused. And all at once she wondered what would happen to the Tucks when her father came. What would he do to them? She would never be able to explain how they had been with her, how they made her feel. She remembered guiltily that at supper she had decided they were criminals. Well, but they *were*. And yet . . .

And then a final visitor made her confusion complete. There was a creaking on the loft stairs and Jesse was looking down at her, very beautiful and eager in the faint blue moonlight. "Hey, Winnie Foster," he whispered. "You asleep?"

This time she sat up, pulling the quilt around her in sudden embarrassment, and answered. "No, not yet."

"Well then, listen." He knelt beside her, his curls tumbled and his eyes wide. "I been thinking it over. Pa's right about you having to keep the secret. It's not hard to see why. But the thing is, you knowing about the water already, and living right next to it so's you could go there any time, well, listen how'd it be if you was to wait till you're seventeen, same age as me—heck, that's only six years off—and then you could go and drink some, and then you could go away with me! We could get married, even. That'd be pretty good, wouldn't it! We could have a grand old time, go all around the world, see everything. Listen, Ma and Pa and Miles, they don't know how to enjoy it, what we got. Why, heck, Winnie, life's to enjoy yourself, isn't it? What else is it good for? That's what *I* say. And you and me, we could have a good time that never, never stopped. Wouldn't that be something?"

Once more Winnie adored him, kneeling there beside her in the moonlight. He wasn't crazy. How could he be? He was just— amazing. But she was struck dumb. All she could do was stare at him.

"You think on it, Winnie Foster," Jesse whispered earnestly. "Think on it some and see if it don't sound good. Anyway, I'll see you in the morning. All right?"

"All right," she managed to whisper in return. He slipped away then, back up the creaking steps, but Winnie sat upright, wide awake, her cheeks burning. She could not deal with this remarkable suggestion, she could not "think on it." For she didn't know what to believe about anything. She lay down again, finally, and stared into the moonlight for another half an hour before she fell asleep.

Chapter 15

IN Treegap, the same moonlight silvered the roof of the touch-me-not cottage, but inside, the lamps were burning. "That's right," said the man in the yellow suit. "I know where she is." He sat back in his chair in the Fosters' spotless parlor, crossing his long, thin legs, and the suspended foot began a rhythmic jiggling.

He hung his hat on his knee and smiled, his eyes nearly closed. "I followed them, you see. She's with them now. As soon as I saw they'd arrived at their destination, I turned around and came directly back. I thought you'd be staying up. You've been looking for her all day, of course. It must be quite a worry."

He lifted a hand then, ignoring their exclamations, and began to smooth the thin hairs of his beard. "You know," he said thoughtfully, "I've come a long way, looking for a wood exactly like the one you've got next door here. It would mean a great deal to me to own it. And how pleasant to have neighbors like yourselves! Now, understand, I wouldn't cut down many of the trees. I'm no barbarian, you can see that. No, just a few. You wouldn't find it different at all, really." He gestured with his long, white fingers and smiled, his face crinkling pleasantly. "We'd be good friends, I think. Why, the little girl and I, we're friends already. It would be a great relief to see her safely home again, wouldn't it?" He clicked his tongue and frowned. "Dreadful thing, kidnapping. Isn't it fortunate that I was a witness! Why, without me, you might never have heard a word. They're rough country people, the ones that took her. There's just no telling what illiterates like that might do. Yes," he sighed, lifting his eyebrows and smiling again, "it looks as if I'm the only person in the whole world who knows where to find her."

And then the man in the yellow suit sat forward. His long face took on a hard expression. "Now, I don't have to spell things out for people like yourselves. Some types one comes across can't seem to cut their way through any problem, and that does make things difficult. But you, I don't have to explain the situation to *you*. I've got what you want, and you've got what I want. Of course, you might find that child without me, but . . . you might not find her in time. So: I want the wood and you want the child. It's a trade. A simple, clear-cut trade."

He looked around at the three shocked faces, and as if he were seeing nothing there but calm agreement, he smiled delightedly and rubbed his hands together. "Done and done," he said. "I knew right away, I said to myself, 'Now here is a group of intelligent, reasonable people!' I'm seldom wrong as a judge of character. Very seldom disappointed. So! All that remains is to write it up on paper, giving me the wood, and to sign it. It's best, don't you agree, to keep things legal and tidy. The rest is easy. Nothing to it. You go for your local constable, and he and I ride out and bring back the child *and* the criminals. No—oh, no, Mr. Foster—I understand your concern, but you mustn't come along. We'll do this business my way. There now! Your terrible ordeal is as good as over, isn't it? I'm so thankful I was here to help you out!"

Chapter 16

THE constable was fat, and he was sleepy. He wheezed when he spoke. And he spoke quite a bit as they started off, he and the man in the yellow suit. "First they roust me out of bed in the middle of the night, after I been out since sun-up looking for that child, and now I s'pose you're going to try to run me all the way," he said sourly. "I got to tell you this horse of mine is none too strong. I don't have to hurry her as a rule, so most of the time it don't matter. Seems to me we could've waited till dawn, anyway."

The man in the yellow suit was as courteous as always. "The Fosters have been waiting since yesterday morning," he pointed out. "Naturally, they're very upset. The sooner we get there, the sooner that child will be with them again."

"How come *you're* so deep in it?" asked the constable suspiciously. "Maybe you're in cahoots with the kidnappers, how do I know? You should of reported it right off, when you saw her get snatched."

The man in the yellow suit sighed. "But of course I had to find out where they were taking her," he explained patiently. "I came right back after that. And the Fosters are friends of mine. They've—uh—sold me their wood."

The constable's eyes went round. "I'll be!" he said. "What do you know about that! I didn't suppose they'd ever do a thing like that, friend or no friend. They're the first family around here, you know. Proud as peacocks, all of 'em. Family-proud, and land-proud, too. But they sold off, did they? Well, well." And he whistled in amazement.

They thumped along in silence for a while, out around the wood and across the star-lit meadow. Then the constable yawned deeply and said, "You ready to tell me how long this is going to take? How far we got to go?"

"Twenty miles north," said the man in the yellow suit.

The constable groaned. "Twenty miles!" He shifted the shotgun that rested across his saddle, and groaned again. "Clear up in the foothills? That's a fair way, all right."

There was no reply to this. The constable ran his fingers down the gleaming barrel of the shotgun. Then he shrugged, and slumped a little in the saddle. "Might as well relax," he wheezed, suddenly companionable. "We'll be riding three, four hours."

Still there was no reply.

"Yessir," said the constable, trying again. "It's something new for these parts, kidnapping. Never had a case like this before that I know of, and I been in charge going on fifteen years."

He waited.

"You don't say so," his companion said at last.

"Yep, that's a fact," said the constable, with evident relief. Maybe now there would be some conversation! "Yep, fifteen years. Seen a lot of trouble in fifteen years, but nothing quite like this. 'Course, there's a first time for everything, as they say. We got a brand-new jailhouse, did you notice? Listen, it's a dandy! Give those folks nice clean accommodations." He chuck-led. "'Course, they won't be there long. Circuit judge'll be com-ing through next week. He'll send 'em over to Charleyville, most likely, to the county jail. That's what they do for your serious crimes. 'Course, we got a gallows of our own, if we ever need it. Keeps down trouble, I think, just having it there. Ain't ever used it yet. That's because they take care of the serious stuff over to Charleyville, like I say."

The constable paused to light a cigar, and went on cheerfully: "What you got planned for that piece of Foster land? Going to clear her? Put up a house, or a store, maybe?"

"No," said the man in the yellow suit.

The constable waited for more, but there was no more. His sour mood returned. He frowned and shook the ashes from his cigar. "Say," he said. "You're kind of a close-lipped feller, ain't you?"

The man in the yellow suit narrowed his eyes. His mouth, above the thin gray beard, twitched with annoyance. "Look here," he said tightly. "Would you mind if I rode on ahead? I'm worried about that child. I'll tell you how to get there, and I'll go on ahead and keep watch."

"Well," said the constable grudgingly, "all right, if you're in such a ding-danged hurry. But don't do nothing till I get there. Those folks are likely dangerous. I'll try to keep up, but this horse of mine, she's none too strong. Don't see as how I could get her to a gallop, even if I tried."

"That's right," said the man in the yellow suit. "So I'll go on ahead, and wait outside the house till you get there."

He explained the route carefully, then dug his heels into the flanks of the fat old horse, cantering off into the darkness where just a hint of dawn glowed on the edges of the hills far ahead.

The constable chewed on the end of his cigar. "Humph," he said to his horse. "Did you get a gander at that suit of clothes? Oh, well, it takes all kinds, as they say." And he followed slowly after, yawning, the gap between him and the man ahead lengthening with every mile.

Chapter 17

FOR the second morning in a row, Winnie Foster woke early. Outside, in the ring of trees around the pond, the birds were celebrating, giving the new day a brass band's worth of greeting. Winnie freed herself from the twisted quilt and went to a window. Mist lay on the surface of the water, and the light was still pale. It looked unreal, and she felt, herself, unreal, waking where she had, with her hair wild and her dress all crumpled. She rubbed her eyes. Through the dewy weeds below the window, a toad hopped suddenly into view and Winnie peered at it eagerly. But no—of course it wasn't the same toad. And remembering that other toad—*her* toad, she thought now, almost fondly—it seemed to her that she had been away from home for weeks. Then she heard a step on the loft stairs and thought, "Jesse!" At once her cheeks flamed.

But it was Miles. He came into the parlor, and when he saw that she was up, he smiled and whispered, "Good! You're awake. Come on—you can help me catch some fish for breakfast."

This time, Winnie was careful not to make a noise when she climbed into the rowboat. She made her way to her seat in the stern, and Miles handed her two old cane poles—"Watch out for the hooks!" he warned—and a jar of bait: pork fat cut into little pieces. A big brown night moth fluttered out from under the oar blades propped beside her on the seat, and wobbled off toward nowhere through the fragrant air. And from the bank, something plopped into the water. A frog! Winnie caught just a glimpse of it as it scissored away from shore. The water was so clear that she could see tiny brown fish near the bottom, flicking this way and that.

Miles pushed the rowboat off and sprang in, and soon they were gliding up toward the near end of the pond, where the water came in from the stream. The locks grated as the oars dipped and swung, but Miles was skillful. He rowed without a single splash. The dripping from the blades, as they lifted, sent rows of overlapping circles spreading silently behind them. It was very peaceful. "They'll take me home today," thought Winnie. She was somehow certain of this, and began to feel quite cheerful. She had been kidnapped, but nothing bad had happened, and now it was almost over. Now, remembering the visits of the night before, she smiled—and found that she loved them, this most peculiar family. They were her friends, after all. And hers alone.

"How'd you sleep?" Miles asked her.

"All right," she said.

"That's good. I'm glad. Ever been fishing before?"

"No," she told him.

"You'll like it. It's fun." And he smiled at her.

The mist was lifting now, as the sun poked up above the trees, and the water sparkled. Miles guided the rowboat near a spot where lily pads lay like upturned palms on the surface. "We'll let her drift some here," he said. "There'll be trout down in those weeds and stems. Here—give me the poles and I'll bait the hooks for us."

Winnie sat watching him as he worked. His face was like Jesse's, and yet not like. It was thinner, without Jesse's rounded cheeks, and paler, and his hair was almost straight, clipped neatly below the ears. His hands were different, too, the fingers thicker, the skin scrubbed-looking, but black at the knuckles and under the nails. Winnie remembered then that he worked sometimes as a blacksmith, and indeed his shoulders, under his threadbare shirt, were broad and muscled. He looked solid, like an oar, whereas Jesse—well, she decided, Jesse was like water: thin, and quick.

Miles seemed to sense that she was watching him. He looked up from the bait jar and his eyes, returning her gaze, were soft. "Remember I told you I had two children?" he asked. "Well, one of 'em was a girl. I took her fishing, too." His face clouded then, and he shook his head. "Her name was Anna. Lord, how sweet she was, that child! It's queer to think she'd be close to eighty now, if she's even still alive. And my son—he'd be eighty-two."

Winnie looked at his young, strong face, and after a moment she said, "Why didn't you take them to the spring and give them some of the special water?"

"Well, of course, we didn't realize about the spring while we was still on the farm," said Miles. "Afterwards, I thought about going to find them. I wanted to, heaven knows. But, Winnie, how'd it have been if I had? My wife was nearly forty by then. And the children—well, what was the use? They'd have been near growed theirselves. They'd have had a pa close to the same age *they* was. No, it'd all have been so mixed up and peculiar, it just wouldn't have worked. Then Pa, he was dead-set against it, anyway. The fewer people know about the spring, he says, the fewer there are to tell about it. Here—here's your pole. Just ease the hook down in the water. You'll know when you get a bite."

Winnie clutched her pole, sitting sidewise in the stern, and watched the baited hook sink slowly down. A dragonfly, a brilliant blue jewel, darted up and paused over the lily pads, then swung up and away. From the nearest bank, a bullfrog spoke.

"There certainly are a lot of frogs around here." Winnie observed.

"That's so," said Miles. "They'll keep coming, too, long as the turtles stay away. Snappers, now, they'll eat a frog soon as look at him."

Winnie thought about this peril to the frogs, and sighed. "It'd be nice," she said, "if nothing ever had to die."

"Well, now, I don't know," said Miles. "If you think on it, you come to see there'd be so many creatures, including people, we'd all be squeezed in right up next to each other before long."

Winnie squinted at her fishing line and tried to picture a teeming world. "Mmm," she said, "yes, I guess you're right."

Suddenly the cane pole jerked in her hands and bent into an arch, its tip dragged down nearly to the water's surface. Winnie held on tight to the handle, her eyes wide.

"Hey!" cried Miles. "Look there! You got a bite. Fresh trout for breakfast, Winnie."

But just as suddenly the pole whipped straight again and the line went slack. "Shucks," said Miles. "It got away."

"I'm kind of glad," Winnie admitted, easing her rigid grip on the butt of the pole. "*You* fish, Miles. I'm not so sure I want to."

And so they drifted for a little longer. The sky was blue and hard now, the last of the mist dissolved, and the sun, stepping higher above the trees, was hot on Winnie's back. The first week of August was reasserting itself after a good night's sleep. It would be another searing day.

A mosquito appeared and sat down on Winnie's knee. She slapped at it absently, thinking about what Miles had said. If all the mosquitoes lived forever—and if they kept on having babies!— it would be terrible. The Tucks were right. It was best if no one knew about the spring, including the mosquitoes. She would keep the secret. She looked at Miles, and then she asked him, "What will you do, if you've got so much time?"

"Someday," said Miles, "I'll find a way to do something important."

Winnie nodded. That was what *she* wanted.

"The way I see it," Miles went on, "it's no good hiding yourself away, like Pa and lots of other people. And it's no good just thinking of your own pleasure, either. People got to do something useful if they're going to take up space in the world."

"But what will you *do?*" Winnie persisted.

"I don't know yet," said Miles. "I ain't had no schooling or nothing, and that makes it harder." Then he set his jaw and added, "I'll find a way, though. I'll locate something."

Winnie nodded. She reached out and ran her fingers across a lily pad that lay on the water beside the boat. It was warm and very dry, like a blotter, but near its center was a single drop of water, round and perfect. She touched the drop and brought her fingertip back wet; but the drop of water, though it rolled a little, remained as round and perfect as before.

And then Miles caught a fish. There it flopped, in the bottom of the boat, its jaw working, its gills fanning rapidly. Winnie drew up her knees and stared at it. It was beautiful, and horrible too, with gleaming, rainbow-colored scales, and an eye like a marble beginning to dim even as she watched it. The hook was caught in its upper lip, and suddenly Winnie wanted to weep. "Put it back, Miles," she said, her voice dry and harsh. "Put it back right away."

Miles started to protest, and then, looking at her face, he picked up the trout and gently worked the barbed hook free. "All right, Winnie," he said. He dropped the fish over the edge of the boat. It flipped its tail and disappeared under the lily pads.

"Will it be all right?" asked Winnie, feeling foolish and happy both at once.

"It'll be all right," Miles assured her. And then he said, "People got to be meat-eaters sometimes, though. It's the natural way. And that means killing things."

"I know," said Winnie weakly. "But still."

"Yes," said Miles. "I know."

Chapter 18

AND so there were flapjacks again for breakfast, but no one seemed to mind. "Didn't get a bite, eh?" said Mae.

"No," said Miles, "nothing we wanted to keep."

That was true, anyway. And though Winnie blushed as he said it, she was grateful that he didn't explain.

"Never mind," said Mae. "You're likely out of practice. Tomorrow, maybe."

"Sure," said Miles. "Tomorrow."

But it was the thought of seeing Jesse again that kept Winnie's stomach fluttering. And at last he came down from the loft, yawning and rosy, rubbing his curls, just as Mae was piling the plates with flapjacks. "Well, slug-a-bed," she said to him fondly. "You come near to missing breakfast. Miles and Winnie been up for hours, out fishing and back already."

"Oh?" said Jesse, his eyes on Miles. "Where's the fish, then? How come we got nothing but flapjacks?"

"No luck," said Mae. "They wasn't biting, for some reason."

"Reason is, Miles don't know how to fish," said Jesse. He grinned at Winnie and she lowered her eyes, her heart thumping.

"It don't matter," said Mae. "We got plenty without. Come and get your plates, everybody."

They sat about in the parlor, as they had the night before. The ceiling swam with bright reflections, and sunlight streamed across the dusty, chip-strewn floor. Mae surveyed it all and sighed contentedly. "Now, this is real nice," she said, her fork poised above her plate. "Everyone sitting down together. And having Winnie here—why, it's just like a party."

"That's the truth," said Jesse and Miles both together, and Winnie felt a rush of happiness.

"Still, we got things to discuss," Tuck reminded them. "There's the business of the horse getting stole. And we got to get Winnie home where she belongs. How we going to do that without the horse?"

"After breakfast, Tuck," said Mae firmly. "Don't spoil a good meal with a lot of talk. We'll get to it soon enough."

So they were silent, eating, and this time Winnie licked the syrup from her fingers without pausing to think about it first. Her fears at last night's supper seemed silly to her now. Perhaps they *were* crazy, but they weren't criminals. She loved them. They belonged to her.

Tuck said, "How'd you sleep, child?"

And she answered, "Just fine," and wished, for a fleeting moment, that she could stay with them forever in that sunny, untidy little house by the pond. Grow up with them and perhaps, if it was true about the spring—then perhaps, when she was seventeen . . . She glanced at Jesse, where he sat on the floor, his

43

curly head bent over his plate. Then she looked at Miles. And then her eyes went to Tuck and lingered on his sad, creased face. It occurred to her that he was the dearest of them all, though she couldn't have explained why she felt that way.

However, there wasn't time to wonder, for at that moment someone knocked at the door.

It was such an alien sound, so sudden and surprising, that Mae dropped her fork, and everyone looked up, startled. "Who's that?" said Tuck.

"I can't imagine," whispered Mae. "We ain't never had callers in all the years we been here."

The knock came again.

"I'll go, Ma," said Miles.

"No, stay where you are," she said. "*I'll* go." She put her plate down carefully on the floor and stood up, straightening her skirts. Then she went to the kitchen and opened the door.

Winnie recognized the voice at once. It was a rich and pleasant voice. The man in the yellow suit. And he was saying, "Good morning, Mrs. Tuck. It *is* Mrs. Tuck, isn't it. May I come in?"

Chapter 19

THE man in the yellow suit came into the sunlit parlor. He stood for a moment, looking around at them all, Mae and Miles and Jesse and Tuck, and Winnie, too. His face was without expression, but there was something unpleasant behind it that Winnie sensed at once, something that made her instantly suspicious. And yet his voice was mild when he said, "You're safe now, Winifred. I've come to take you home."

"We was going to bring her back directly, ourself," said Tuck, standing up slowly. "She ain't been in no danger."

"You're Mr. Tuck, I suppose," said the man in the yellow suit.

"I am," said Tuck formally, his back straighter than usual.

"Well, you may as well sit down again. You, too, Mrs. Tuck. I have a great deal to say and very little time for saying it."

Mae sat down on the edge of the rocker, and Tuck sat, too, but his eyes were narrowed.

Jesse said, uneasily, "Who in tarnation do you think you—"

But Tuck interrupted. "Hush, boy. Let him speak his piece."

"That's wise," said the man in the yellow suit. "I'll be as brief as possible." He took off his hat and laid it on the mantel, and then he stood tapping his foot on the littered hearth, facing them. His face was smooth and empty. "I was born west of here," he began, "and all the time I was growing up, my grandmother told me stories. They were wild, unbelievable stories, but *I* believed them. They involved a dear friend of my grandmother's who married into a very odd family. Married the older of two sons, and they had two children. It was after the children were born that she began to see that the family was odd. This friend of my grandmother's, she lived with her husband for twenty years, and strange to say, he never got any older. *She* did, but he didn't. And neither did his mother or his father or his brother. People began to wonder about that family, and my grandmother's friend decided at last that they were witches, or worse. She left her husband and came with her children to live at my grandmother's house for a short while. Then she moved west. I don't know what became of her. But my mother still remembers playing with the children. They were all about the same age. There was a son, and a daughter."

"Anna!" whispered Miles.

Mae burst out, "You got no call to come and bring us pain!"

And Tuck added roughly, "You got something to say, you better come to the point and say it."

"There, there, now," said the man in the yellow suit. He spread his long, white fingers in a soothing gesture. "Hear me out. As I've told you, I was fascinated by my grandmother's stories. People who never grew older! It was fantastic. It took possession of me. I decided to devote my life to finding out if it could be true, and if so, how and why. I went to school, I went to a university, I studied philosophy, metaphysics, even a little medicine. None of it did me any good. Oh, there were ancient legends, but nothing more. I nearly gave it up. It began to seem ridiculous, and a waste of time. I went home. My grandmother was very old by then. I took her a present one day, a music box. And when I gave it to her, it reminded her of something: the woman, the mother of the family that didn't grow old, *she* had had a music box."

Mae's hand went to the pocket of her skirt. Her mouth opened, and then she shut it again with a snap.

"That music box played a very particular tune," the man in the yellow suit went on. "My grandmother's friend and her children—Anna? Was that the daughter's name?—they'd heard it so often that they knew it by heart. They'd taught it to my mother during the short time they lived in the house. We talked about it then, all those years afterward, my mother, my grandmother, and I. My mother was able to remember the melody, finally. She taught it to me. That was nearly twenty years ago now, but I kept it in my head. It was a clue."

The man in the yellow suit folded his arms and rocked a little. His voice was easy, almost friendly. "During those twenty years," he said, "I worked at other things. But I couldn't forget the tune or the family that didn't grow older. They haunted my dreams. So a few months ago I left my home and I started out to look for them, following the route they were said to have taken when they left their farm. No one I asked along the way knew anything. No one had heard of them, no one recognized their name. But two evenings ago, I heard that music box, I heard that very tune, and it was coming from the Fosters' wood. And next morning early, I saw the family at last, taking Winifred away. I followed, and I heard their story, every word."

Mae's face drained of color. Her mouth hung open. And Tuck said hoarsely, "What you going to do?"

The man in the yellow suit smiled. "The Fosters have given me the wood," he said. "In exchange for bringing Winifred home. I was the only one who knew where she was, you see. So it was a trade. Yes, I followed you, Mrs. Tuck, and then I took your horse and went directly back."

The tension in the parlor was immense. Winnie found that she could scarcely breathe. It *was* true, then! Or was the man who stood there crazy, too?

"Horse thief!" cried Tuck. "Get to the point! What you going to do?"

"It's very simple," said the man in the yellow suit. And, as he said this, the smoothness of his face began to loosen a little. A faint flush crept up his neck, and the pitch of his voice lifted, became a fraction higher. "Like all magnificent things, it's very simple. The wood—and the spring—belong to me now." He patted his breast pocket. "I have a paper here, all signed and legal, to prove it. I'm going to sell the water, you see."

"You can't do that!" roared Tuck. "You got to be out of your mind!"

The man in the yellow suit frowned. "But I'm not going to sell it to just anybody," he protested. "Only to certain people, people who deserve it. And it will be very, very expensive. But who wouldn't give a fortune to live forever?"

"I wouldn't," said Tuck grimly.

"Exactly," said the man in the yellow suit. His eyes glowed. "Ignorant people like you should never have the opportunity. It should be kept for . . . certain others. And for me. However, since it's already too late to keep you out, you may as well join me in what I'm going to do. You can show me where the spring is and help me to advertise. We'll set up demonstrations. You know—things that would be fatal to anybody else, but won't affect you in the least. I'll pay for your assistance, of course. It won't take long for the word to spread. And then you can go your way. Well, what do you say?"

Jesse said dully, "Freaks. You want us to be freaks. In a patent-medicine show."

The man in the yellow suit raised his eyebrows and a nervous petulance came into his voice. "Of course, if the idea doesn't appeal to you," he said, blinking rapidly, "you needn't be in on it. I can find the spring and manage just as well without you. But it seemed the gentlemanly thing to make the offer. After all," he added, looking round at the cluttered room, "it would mean you could afford to live like people again, instead of pigs."

And that was when the tension burst. All four Tucks sprang to their feet at once, while Winnie, very frightened, shrank back in her chair. Tuck cried, "You're a madman! A loony! You can't let *no* one know about that water. Don't you see what would *happen?*"

"I've given you your chance," shrilled the man in the yellow suit, "and you've refused it." He seized Winnie roughly by the arm and dragged her up out of her chair. "I'll take the child, and be on about my business."

Tuck began to rave now, his face stretched with horror. "Madman!" he shouted. And Miles and Jesse began to shout, too. They crowded after as the man in the yellow suit dragged Winnie through the kitchen to the door.

"No!" she was screaming, for now at last she hated him. "I won't go with you! I won't!"

But he opened the door and pushed her out in front of him. His eyes were like blind firepoints, his face was twisted.

Then the shouting behind them stopped abruptly, and in the midst of the sudden silence came Mae's voice, flat and cold. "You leave that child be," she said.

Winnie stared. Mae was standing just outside the doorway. She held Tuck's long-forgotten shotgun by the barrel, like a club.

The man in the yellow suit smiled a ghastly smile. "I can't think why you're so upset. Did you really believe you could keep that water for yourselves? Your selfishness is really quite extraordinary, and worse than that, you're stupid. You could have done what I'm about to do, long ago. Now it's too late. Once Winifred drinks some of the water, she'll do just as well for my demonstrations. Even better. Children are much more appealing, anyway. So you may as well relax. There's nothing you can do to stop me."

But he was wrong. Mae lifted the shotgun. Behind her, Miles gasped, "Ma! *No!*"

But Mae's face was dark red. "Not Winnie!" she said between clenched teeth. "You ain't going to do a thing like that to Winnie. And you ain't going to give out the secret." Her strong arms swung the shotgun round her head, like a wheel. The man in the yellow suit jerked away, but it was too late. With a dull cracking sound, the stock of the shotgun smashed into the back of his skull. He dropped like a tree, his face surprised, his eyes wide open. And at that very moment, riding through the pine trees just in time to see it all, came the Treegap constable.

Chapter 20

WINNIE was standing with her cheek pressed into Tuck's chest, her arms flung tight around him. She trembled, and kept her eyes squeezed shut. She could feel Tuck's breath come and go in little gasps. It was very quiet.

The Treegap constable knelt over the sprawled body of the man in the yellow suit, and then he said, "He ain't dead. Leastways, not yet."

Winnie opened her eyes a crack. She could see the shotgun lying on the grass where Mae had dropped it. She could see Mae's hands, too, hanging limp, clenching, then hanging limp again. The sun was scorching hot, and near her ear a gnat whined.

The constable stood up. "What did you hit him for?" he wheezed resentfully.

"He was taking the child away," said Mae. Her voice was dull and exhausted. "He was taking the child against her will."

At this the constable exploded. "Ding-dang it, woman, what you trying to say? Taking that child against her will? That's what *you* done. You *kidnapped* that child."

Winnie let go of Tuck's waist and turned around. Her trembling had stopped. "They didn't kidnap me," she said. "I came because I wanted to."

Behind her, Tuck drew his breath in sharply.

"You wanted to?" echoed the constable, his eyes wide with disbelief. "You *wanted* to?"

"That's right," said Winnie unflinchingly. "They're my friends."

The constable stared at her. He scratched his chin, eyebrows high, and eased his own shotgun to the ground. Then he shrugged and looked down at the man in the yellow suit, who lay motionless on the grass, the blazing sun white on his face and hands. His eyes were closed now, but except for that, he looked more than ever like a marionette, a marionette flung carelessly into a corner, arms and legs every which way midst tangled strings.

The one glance she gave him fixed his appearance forever in Winnie's mind. She turned her eyes away quickly, looking to Tuck for relief. But Tuck was not looking back at her. Instead, he was gazing at the body on the ground, leaning forward slightly, his brows drawn down, his mouth a little open. It was as if he were entranced and—yes, envious—like a starving man looking through a window at a banquet. Winnie could not bear to see him like that. She reached out a hand and touched him, and it broke the spell. He blinked and took her hand, squeezing it.

"Well, anyway," said the constable at last, turning businesslike, "I got to take charge here. Get this feller into the house before he fries. I'm telling you now: if he don't make it, you're in a pickle, you people. Now, here's what we'll do. You," he said, pointing at Mae, "you got to come with me, you and the little girl. You got to be locked up right away; and the little girl, I got to get her home. The rest of you, you stay here with him. Look after him. I'll get back with a doctor quick as I can. Should have brought a deputy, but I didn't expect nothing like this to happen. Well, it's too late now. All right, let's get moving."

Miles said softly, "Ma. We'll get you out right away."

"Sure, Ma," said Jesse.

"Don't worry about me none," said Mae in the same exhausted voice. "I'll make out."

"Make out?" exclaimed the constable. "You people beat all. If this feller dies, you'll get the gallows, that's what you'll get, if that's what you mean by make out."

Tuck's face crumpled. "The gallows?" he whispered. "Hanging?"

"That's it," said the constable. "That's the law. Now, let's get going."

Miles and Jesse lifted the man in the yellow suit and carried him carefully into the house, but Tuck stood staring, and Winnie could guess what he was thinking. The constable swung her up onto his horse and directed Mae to her own saddle. But Winnie kept her eyes on Tuck. His face was very pale, the creases deeper than ever, and his eyes looked blank and sunken. She heard him whisper again, "The gallows!"

And then Winnie said something she had never said before, but the words were words she had sometimes heard, and often longed to hear. They sounded strange on her own lips and made her sit up straighter. "Mr. Tuck," she said, "don't worry. Everything's going to be all right."

The constable glanced heavenward and shook his head. Then, clutching his shotgun, he climbed up behind Winnie and turned the horse toward the path. "You first," he barked at Mae. "I got to keep an eye on you. And as for you," he added grimly, speaking to Tuck, "you better hope that feller don't die on you. I'll be back soon as I can."

"Everything'll be all right," Tuck repeated slowly.

Mae, slumped on the back of the fat old horse, did not respond. But Winnie leaned round the constable and looked back at Tuck. "You'll see," she said. And then she faced forward, sitting very straight. She was going home, but the thought of that was far from her mind. She watched the rump of the horse ahead, the swish of coarse, dusty hairs as he moved his tail. And she watched the swaying, sagging back of the woman who rode him.

Up through the dim pine trees they went, the constable's breath wheezing in her ears, and emerging from the coolness and the green, Winnie saw again the wide world spread before her, shimmering with light and possibility. But the possibilities were different now. They did not point to what might happen to her but to what she herself might keep from happening. For the only thing she could think of was the clear and terrible necessity: Mae Tuck must never go to the gallows. Whatever happened to the man in the yellow suit, Mae Tuck must not be hanged. Because if all they had said was true, then Mae, even if she were the cruelest of murderers and deserved to be put to death—Mae Tuck would not be able to die.

Chapter 21

WINNIE pulled her little rocking chair up to her bedroom window and sat down. The rocking chair had been given to her when she was very small, but she still squeezed into it sometimes, when no one was looking, because the rocking made her almost remember something pleasant, something soothing, that would never quite come up to the surface of her mind. And tonight she wanted to be soothed.

The constable had brought her home. They had seized her at once, flinging the gate open and swooping down on her, her mother weeping, her father speechless, hugging her to him, her grandmother babbling with excitement. There was a painful pause when the constable told them she had gone away of her own free will, but it only lasted for a moment. They did not, would not believe it, and her grandmother said, "It was the elves. We heard them. They must have bewitched her."

And so they had borne her into the house, and after she had taken the bath they insisted upon, they fed and petted her and refused, with little laughs and murmurs, to accept her answers to their questions: She had gone away with the Tucks because—well, she just wanted to. The Tucks had been very kind to her, had given her flapjacks, taken her fishing. The Tucks were good and gentle people. All this would have been swept away in any case, however, this good impression of her friends which she was trying to create, when she told them what had happened to the man in the yellow suit. Had they really given him the wood in exchange for finding her? They had. Well, perhaps he wouldn't want it now. Mae had hit him with the shotgun. He was very sick. They received this news with mingled hope and horror, and her father said, "I suppose the wood will be ours again if that man should . . . that is, if he doesn't . . ."

"You mean, if he dies," Winnie had said, flatly, and they had sat back, shocked. Soon after, they put her to bed, with many kisses. But they peered at her anxiously over their shoulders as they tiptoed out of her bedroom, as if they sensed that she was different now from what she had been before. As if some part of her had slipped away.

Well, thought Winnie, crossing her arms on the windowsill, she *was* different. Things had happened to her that were hers alone, and had nothing to do with them. It was the first time. And no amount of telling about it could help them understand or share what she felt. It was satisfying and lonely, both at once. She rocked, gazing out at the twilight, and the soothing feeling came reliably into her bones. That feeling—it tied her to them, to her mother, her father, her grandmother, with strong threads too ancient and precious to be broken. But there were new threads now, tugging and insistent, which tied her just as firmly to the Tucks.

Winnie watched the sky slide into blackness over the wood

outside her window. There was not the least hint of a breeze to soften the heavy August night. And then, over the treetops, on the faraway horizon, there was a flash of white. Heat lightning. Again and again it throbbed, without a sound. It was like pain, she thought. And suddenly she longed for a thunderstorm.

She cradled her head in her arms and closed her eyes. At once the image of the man in the yellow suit rose up. She could see him again, sprawled motionless on the sun-blanched grass. "He can't die," she whispered, thinking of Mae. "He mustn't." And then she considered his plans for the water in the spring, and Tuck's voice saying, "They'd all come running like pigs to slops." And she found herself thinking, "If it's true about the spring, then he has to die. He must. And that's why she did it."

Then she heard hoofbeats on the road below, a horse hurrying into the village, and not long after, there were footsteps and a knocking on the door. Winnie crept out of her room and crouched in the shadows at the top of the stairs. It was the constable. She heard him saying, "So that's that, Mr. Foster. We can't press no kidnapping charges, since your little girl claims there *wasn't* no kidnapping. But it don't matter now, anyway. The doc just got back a few minutes ago. That feller—the one you sold your land to? He's dead." There was a pause, and the murmur of other voices; then a match striking, the acrid smell of fresh cigar smoke. "Yep, she got him a good one, all right. He never even come to. So it's an open-and-shut case, since I seen her do it. Eyewitness. No question about it. They'll hang her for sure."

Winnie went back to her room and climbed into bed. She lay in the dark, propped up on the pillows, and stared at the lighter square of her window, at the heat lightning throbbing. It was like pain, she thought again, a dull pain on the fringes of the sky. Mae had killed the man in the yellow suit. And she had meant to kill him.

Winnie had killed a wasp once, in fear and anger, just in time to spare herself a stinging. She had slammed at the wasp with a heavy book, and killed it. And then, seeing its body broken, the thin wings stilled, she had wished it were alive again. She had wept for that wasp. Was Mae weeping now for the man in the yellow suit? In spite of her wish to spare the world, did she wish he were alive again? There was no way of knowing. But Mae had done what she thought she had to do. Winnie closed her eyes to shut out the silent pulsing of the lightning. Now *she* would have to do something. She had no idea what, but something. Mae Tuck must not go to the gallows.

Chapter 22

NEXT morning Winnie went out to the fence directly after breakfast. It was the hottest day yet, so heavy that the slightest exertion brought on a flood of perspiration, an exhaustion in the joints. Two days before, they would have insisted that she stay indoors, but now, this morning, they were careful with her, a little gingerly, as if she were an egg. She had said, "I'm going outside now," and they had said, "All right, but come in if it gets too hot, won't you, dear?" And she had answered, "Yes."

The earth, where it was worn bald under the gate, was cracked, and hard as rock, a lifeless tan color; and the road was an aisle of brilliant velvet dust. Winnie leaned against the fence, her hands gripping the warm metal of the bars, and thought about Mae behind another set of bars in the jailhouse. And then, lifting her head, she saw the toad. It was squatting where she had seen it first, across the road. "Hello!" she said, very glad to see it.

The toad did not so much as flick a muscle or blink an eye. It looked dried out today, parched. "It's thirsty," said Winnie to herself. "No wonder, on a day like this." She left the fence and went back into the cottage. "Granny, can I have some water in a dish? There's a toad out front that looks as if he's just about to die of thirst."

"A toad?" said her grandmother, wrinkling her nose in disgust. "Nasty things, toads."

"Not this one," said Winnie. "This one is always out there, and I like him. Can I give him a drink of water?"

"Toads don't drink water, Winifred. It wouldn't do him any good."

"They don't drink water at all?"

"No. They take it in through their skins, like a sponge. When it rains."

"But it hasn't rained forever!" said Winnie, alarmed. "I could sprinkle some water on him, couldn't I? That would help, wouldn't it?"

"Well, I suppose so," said her grandmother. "Where is he? In the yard?"

"No," said Winnie. "He's across the road."

"I'll come with you, then. I don't want you leaving the yard alone."

But when they came out to the fence, Winnie balancing a small bowl of water with enormous care, the toad was gone.

"Well, he must be all right," said her grandmother. "If he could hop off."

With mingled disappointment and relief, Winnie tipped the water onto the cracked earth at the gate. It was sucked in immediately, and the wet brown stain it left behind paled and vanished almost as quickly.

"I never saw such heat in all my life," said Winnie's grandmother, dabbing uselessly at her neck with a handkerchief. "Don't stay out here much longer."

"I won't," said Winnie, and was left alone once more. She sat down on the grass and sighed. Mae! What could she do to set Mae free? She closed her eyes against the glaring light, and watched, a little dizzily, as brilliant patterns of red and orange danced inside her eyelids.

And then, miraculously, Jesse was there, crouching just on the other side of the fence. "Winnie!" he hissed. "You sleeping?"

"Oh, Jesse!" Her eyes flew open and she reached through the fence to grasp his hand. "I'm so glad to see you! What can we do? We have to get her out!"

"Miles's got a plan, but I don't see how it can work," said Jesse, speaking quickly, his voice almost a whisper. "He knows a lot about carpentering. He says he can take Ma's window frame right straight out of the wall, bars and all, and she can climb through. We're going to try it tonight when it gets dark. Only trouble is, that constable keeps watching her every minute, he's so durned proud of having a prisoner in that new jail of his. We been down to see her. She's all right. But even if she can climb through the window, he'll come after her soon's he sees she's gone. Seems to me he'll notice right off. That don't give us much time to get away. But we got to try it. There ain't no other way. Anyhow, I come to say goodbye. We won't be able to come back here for a long, long time, Winnie, if we get away. I mean, they'll be looking for Ma. Winnie, listen—I won't see you again, not for ages. Look now—here's a bottle of water from the spring. You keep it. And then, no matter where you are, when you're seventeen, Winnie, you can drink it, and then come find us. We'll leave directions somehow. Winnie, please say you will!"

He pressed the little bottle into her hands and Winnie took it, closing her fingers over it. "Jesse, wait!" she whispered breathlessly, for all at once she had the answer. "I can help! When your mother climbs out the window, I'll climb in and take her place. I can wrap myself up in her blanket, and when the constable looks in, he won't be able to tell the difference. Not in the dark. I can hump up and look a lot bigger. Miles can even put the window back. That would give you time to get away! You'd have at least till morning!"

Jesse squinted at her, and then he said, "Yep—you know, it might work. It might just make the difference. But I don't know as Pa's going to want you taking any risk. I mean, what'll they say to you after, when they find out?"

"I don't know," said Winnie, "but it doesn't matter. Tell your father I want to help. I *have* to help. If it wasn't for me, there wouldn't have been any trouble in the first place. Tell him I have to."

"Well . . . all right. Can you get out after dark?"

"Yes," said Winnie.

"Then—at midnight, Winnie. I'll be waiting for you right here at midnight."

"Winifred!" an anxious voice called from the cottage. "Who's that you're talking to?"

Winnie stood up and turned to answer. "It's just a boy, Granny. I'll be in in a minute." When she turned around again, Jesse was gone. Winnie clutched the little bottle in her hands and tried to control the rising excitement that made her breath catch. At midnight she would make a difference in the world.

Chapter 23

IT was the longest day: mindlessly hot, unspeakably hot, too hot to move or even think. The countryside, the village of Treegap, the wood—all lay defeated. Nothing stirred. The sun was a ponderous circle without edges, a roar without a sound, a blazing glare so thorough and remorseless that even in the Fosters' parlor, with curtains drawn, it seemed an actual presence. You could not shut it out.

Winnie's mother and grandmother sat plaintive all afternoon in the parlor, fanning themselves and sipping lemonade, their hair unsettled and their knees loose. It was totally unlike them, this lapse from gentility, and it made them much more interesting. But Winnie didn't stay with them. Instead, she took her own brimming glass to her room and sat in her little rocker by the window. Once she had hidden Jesse's bottle in a bureau drawer, there was nothing to do but wait. In the hall outside her room, the grandfather's clock ticked deliberately, unimpressed with anyone's impatience, and Winnie found herself rocking to its rhythm—forward, back, forward, back, tick, tock, tick, tock. She tried to read, but it was so quiet that she could not concentrate, and so she was glad when at last it was time for supper. It was something to do, though none of them could manage more than a nibble.

But later, when Winnie went out again to the fence, she saw that the sky was changing. It was not so much clouding up as thickening, somehow, from every direction at once, the blank blue gone to haze. And then, as the sun sank reluctantly behind the treetops, the haze hardened to a brilliant brownish-yellow. In the wood, the leaves turned underside-up, giving the trees a silvery cast.

The air was noticeably heavier. It pressed on Winnie's chest and made her breathing difficult. She turned and went back into the cottage. "It's going to rain, I think," she told the prostrate group in the parlor, and the news was received with little moans of gratitude.

Everyone went to bed early, closing windows firmly on their way. For outside, though it was almost dark, shreds of the hard brown-yellow light lingered on the rims of things, and there was a wind beginning, small gusts that rattled the fence gate and set the trees to rustling. The smell of rain hung sweet in the air. "What a week *this* has been!" said Winnie's grandmother. "Well, thank the Lord, it's almost over." And Winnie thought to herself: Yes, it's almost over.

There were three hours to wait before midnight and nothing whatever to do. Winnie wandered restlessly about her room, sat in her rocker, lay on her bed, counted the ticks of the hall clock. Beneath her excitement, she was thick with guilt. For the second time in three short days—though they seemed many more than that—she was about to do something which she knew would be forbidden. She didn't have to ask.

Winnie had her own strong sense of rightness. She knew that she could always say, afterward, "Well, you never told me *not* to!" But how silly that would be! Of course it would never occur to them to include such a thing on their list of don'ts. She could hear them saying it, and almost smiled: "Now, remember, Winifred—don't bite your fingernails, don't interrupt when someone else is speaking, and don't go down to the jailhouse at midnight to change places with prisoners."

Still, it wasn't really funny. What would happen in the morning, when the constable found her in the cell and had to bring her home for the second time? What would they say? Would they ever trust her again? Winnie squirmed, sitting in the rocker, and swallowed uncomfortably. Well, she would have to make them understand, somehow, without explaining.

The hall clock chimed eleven. Outside, the wind had stopped.

Everything, it seemed, was waiting. Winnie lay down and closed her eyes. Thinking of Tuck and Mae, of Miles and Jesse, her heart softened. They needed her. To take care of them. For in the funny sort of way that had struck her at the first, they were helpless. Or too trusting. Well, *something* like that. Anyway, they needed her. She would not disappoint them. Mae would go free. No one would have to find out—Winnie would not have to find out—that Mae could not . . . but Winnie blocked the picture from her mind, the horror that would prove the secret. Instead, she turned her thoughts to Jesse. When she was seventeen— would she? If it was true, would she? And if she did, would she be sorry afterwards? Tuck had said, "It's something you don't find out how you feel until afterwards." But no—it wasn't true. She knew that, now, here in her own bedroom. They were probably crazy after all. But she loved them anyway. They needed her. And, thinking this, Winnie fell asleep.

She woke with a jerk sometime later, and sat up, alarmed. The clock was ticking steadily, the darkness was complete. Outside, the night seemed poised on tiptoe, waiting, waiting, holding its breath for the storm. Winnie stole out to the hall and frowned at the clock face in the shadows. And at last she could make it out, for the black Roman numerals were just barely visible against their white ground, the brass hands glowed faintly. As she peered at them, the long hand snapped forward one more notch, with a loud click. She had not missed her moment—it was five minutes to midnight.

Chapter 24

LEAVING the house was so easy that Winnie felt faintly shocked. She had half expected that the instant she put a foot on the stairs they would leap from their beds and surround her with accusations. But no one stirred. And she was struck by the realization that, if she chose, she could slip out night after night without their knowing. The thought made her feel more guilty than ever that she should once more take advantage of their trust. But tonight, this one last time, she had to. There was no other way. She opened the door and slipped out into the heavy August night.

Leaving the cottage was like leaving something real and moving into dream. Her body felt weightless, and she seemed to float down the path to the gate. Jesse was there, waiting. Neither of them spoke. He took her hand and they ran together, lightly, down the road, past other sleeping cottages, into the dim and empty center of the village. The big glass windows here were lidded eyes that didn't care—that barely saw them, barely gave them back reflections. The blacksmith's shop, the mill, the church, the stores, so busy and alive in daylight, were hunched, deserted now, dark piles and shapes without a purpose or a meaning. And then, ahead, Winnie saw the jailhouse, its new wood still unpainted, lamplight spilling through a window at the front. And there, in the cleared yard behind it, like a great L upside down, was the gallows.

The sky flashed white. But this time it wasn't heat lightning, for a few moments later a low mumble, still far away, announced at last the coming storm. A fresh breeze lifted Winnie's hair, and from somewhere in the village behind them a dog barked.

Two shadows detached themselves from the gloom as Winnie and Jesse came up. Tuck pulled her to him and hugged her hard, and Miles squeezed her hand. No one said a word. Then the four of them crept to the back of the building. Here, too high for Winnie to see into, was a barred window through which, from the room in front, light glowed faintly. Winnie peered up at it, at the blackness of the bars with the dim gold of the light between. Into her head came lines from an old poem:

> *Stone walls do not a prison make,*
> *Nor iron bars a cage.*

Over and over the lines repeated themselves in her head till they were altogether meaningless. Another roll of thunder sounded. The storm was moving nearer.

Then Miles was standing on a box. He was pouring oil around the frame of the window. A swirl of wind brought the thick, rich smell of it down to Winnie's nostrils. Tuck handed up a tool and Miles began to pry at the nails securing the window frame. Miles knew carpentering. Miles could do the job. Winnie shivered and held tight to Jesse's hand. One nail was free. Another. Tuck reached up to receive them as they came out one by one. A fourth nail screeched as it was pried up, and Miles poured on more oil.

From the front of the jailhouse, the constable yawned noisily and began to whistle. The whistling came nearer. Miles dropped down. They heard the constable's footsteps coming up to Mae's cell. The barred door clanked. Then the footsteps receded, the whistling grew fainter. An inner door shut, and the lamp glow disappeared.

At once Miles was up again and prying at the nails. An eighth was out, a ninth, a tenth. Winnie counted carefully, while behind her counting, her mind sang, "Stone walls do not a prison make."

Miles handed down the prying tool. He grasped the bars of the window firmly, ready to pull, and stood poised. "What is he waiting for?" thought Winnie. "Why doesn't he . . ." Then—a flash of lightning and, soon after, a crack of thunder. In the midst of the noise, Miles gave a mighty heave. But the window did not budge.

The thunder ebbed. Winnie's heart sank. What if it was all impossible? What if the window would never come out? What if . . . She looked over her shoulder at the dark shape of the gallows, and shuddered.

Again a flash of lightning, and this time a crashing burst of noise from the swirling sky. Miles yanked. The window frame sprang free, and still grasping it by the bars, he tumbled backward off the box. The job was done.

Two arms appeared in the hole left by the missing frame. Mae! Her head appeared. It was too dark to see her face. The window—what if it was too small for her to squeeze through? What if . . . But now her shoulders were out. She groaned softly. Another flash of lighting lit her face for an instant and Winnie saw an expression there of deep concentration, tip of tongue protruding, brows furrowed.

Now Tuck was on the box, helping her, giving her his own shoulders to pull on, Miles and Jesse close at his sides, arms upstretched, eager to receive her bulk. Her hips were free—now, look out!—here she came, her skirts tearing on the rough edges of the boards, arms flailing—and they were all in a heap on the ground. Another crash of thunder muffled Jesse's bursting, exultant laugh. Mae was free.

Winnie clasped her trembling hands thankfully. And then the first drop of rain plopped precisely on the tip of her nose. The Tucks untangled themselves and turned to her. One by one, as the rain began, they drew her to them and kissed her. One by one she kissed them back. Was it rain on Mae's face? On Tuck's? Or was it tears? Jesse was last. He put his arms around her and hugged her tight, and whispered the single word, "Remember!"

Then Miles was on the box again, lifting her. Her hands grasped the edges of the window. This time she waited with him. When the thunder came, it tore the sky apart with its roar, and as it came, she pulled herself through, and dropped to the cot inside, unharmed. She looked up at the open square and saw the frame with Miles's hands holding it. The next obliging roll of thunder saw it wedged once more into place. And then—would Miles put back the nails? She waited.

Rain came in sheets now, riding the wind, flung crosswise through the night. Lightning crackled, a brilliant, jagged streak, and thunder rattled the little building. The tension in the parched earth eased and vanished. Winnie felt it go. The muscles of her stomach loosened, and all at once she was exhausted.

Still she waited. Would Miles put back the nails? At last, standing tiptoe on the cot, she grasped the bars of the window, pulling herself up till she could just see through. Rain blew into her face, but at the next flash of lightning, looking down, she saw that the yard was empty. And before the thunder followed, in a pause while wind and rain held back for one brief moment, she thought she heard, fading in the distance, the tinkling little melody of the music box. The Tucks—her darling Tucks—were gone.

Chapter 25

THE first week of August was long over. And now, though autumn was still some weeks away, there was a feeling that the year had begun its downward arc, that the wheel was turning again, slowly now, but soon to go faster, turning once more in its changeless sweep of change. Winnie, standing at the fence in front of the touch-me-not cottage, could hear the new note in the voices of the birds. Whole clouds of them lifted, chattering, into the sky above the wood, and then settled, only to lift again. Across the road, goldenrod was coming into bloom. And an early-drying milkweed had opened its rough pod, exposing a host of downy-headed seeds. As she watched, one of these detached itself into a sudden breeze and sailed sedately off, while others leaned from the pod as if to observe its departure.

Winnie dropped down cross-legged on the grass. Two weeks had gone by since the night of the storm, the night of Mae Tuck's escape. And Mae had not been found. There was no trace of her at all, or of Tuck or Miles or Jesse. Winnie was profoundly grateful for that. But she was also profoundly tired. It had been a trying two weeks.

For the hundredth time she reviewed it all: how the constable had come into the cell soon after she had settled herself on the cot; how he had let down a shutter over the window to keep out the rain; how, then, he had stood over her as she hunched under the blanket, her breath heavy, trying to look as large as possible; how, finally, he had gone away and not come back till morning.

But she had not dared to sleep, for fear she would kick off the blanket and give herself away—give the Tucks away—unwittingly. So she had lain there, pulse thudding, eyes wide open. She would never forget the rattle of the rain on the jailhouse roof, or the smell of wet wood, or the darkness that had saved them all, or how difficult it was not to cough. She had wanted to cough as soon as it occurred to her that she mustn't, and she passed a long hour trying to swallow away the tickle that perversely constricted her throat. And she would never forget the crash outside that made her heart race, that she could not investigate, and did not understand till morning, when on the way home she saw that the gallows had blown over in the wind.

But oh!—it made her tremble still to remember the constable's face when he found her. She had heard first a bustling in the front of the jail, and smelled fresh coffee, and had sat up, stiff with apprehension. Then the inner door opened—the door, she now saw, which separated the office from the pair of cells— and in the light that streamed before him, the constable appeared, carrying a breakfast tray. He was whistling cheerfully. He came up to the barred door of her cell and looked in. And his whistling died on his lips as if it had run down and needed to be wound up again. But this comical astonishment lasted for a moment only. And then his face flushed red with anger.

Winnie had sat on the cot, eyes downcast, feeling very small— and very like a criminal. In fact, he was soon shouting that if she were older, he'd have to keep her there—that it *was* a crime, what she had done. She was . . . an accomplice. She had helped a murderer escape. She was, in fact, a criminal. But too young to be punished by the law. Worse luck, he told her, for she badly needed punishing.

She was released, then, into the custody of her mother and father. And these new words, "accomplice" and "custody," chilled her blood. Over and over they asked her, shocked at first and then wistful: why had she *done* such a thing? *Why?* She was their daughter. They had trusted her. They had tried to bring her up properly, with a true sense of right and wrong. They did not understand. And finally she had sobbed the only truth there was into her mother's shoulder, the only explanation: the Tucks were her friends. She had done it because—in spite of everything, she loved them.

This of all things her family understood, and afterward they drew together staunchly around her. It was hard for them in the village, Winnie knew it was, and the knowledge gave her pain. For they were proud. And she had shamed them. Still, this side of the affair was not without its benefits, at least for Winnie. Though she was confined to the yard indefinitely and could go nowhere, not even with her mother or her grandmother, the other children wandered by to look at her, to talk to her through the fence. They were impressed by what she had done. She was a figure of romance to them now, where before she had been too neat, too prissy; almost, somehow, too *clean* to be a real friend.

Winnie sighed and plucked at the grass around her ankles. School would open soon. It wouldn't be so bad. In fact, she thought as her spirits lifted, this year it might be rather nice.

And then two things happened. First of all, the toad appeared out of the weeds, on her side of the road this time. It bounced out of a cover of old dandelion leaves and landed—plop!—just beyond the fence. If she had reached her hand through the bars, she could have touched it. And next, a large brown dog, with easy gait and dangling tongue, came loping down the road toward them. He stopped opposite the fence and looked at Winnie with a friendly swish of his tail, and then he saw the toad. At once he began to bark, his eyes bright. He pranced up, his hind quarters leaping independently from side to side, nose close to the toad, his voice shrill with enthusiasm.

"Don't!" cried Winnie, leaping to her feet and flapping her arms. "Go away, dog! Stop that! Go away—shoo!"

The dog paused. He looked up at Winnie's frantic dancing and then he looked at the toad, who had pressed down close to the dirt, eyes tight shut. It was too much for him. He began to bark again, and reached out a long paw.

"Oh!" cried Winnie. "Oh—*don't* do that! Leave my toad *alone!*" And before she had time to realize what she was doing, she bent, reached through the bars, and snatched the toad up and away from harm, dropping it on the grass inside the fence.

A feeling of revulsion swept through her. While the dog whined, pawing uselessly at the fence, she stood rigid, staring at the toad, wiping her hand again and again on the skirt of her dress. Then she remembered the actual feel of the toad, and the revulsion passed. She knelt and touched the skin of its back. It was rough and soft, both at once. And cool.

Winnie stood up and looked at the dog. He was waiting outside the fence, his head on one side, peering at her longingly. "It's *my* toad," Winnie told him. "So you'd better leave it alone." And then, on an impulse, she turned and ran into the cottage, up to her room, to the bureau drawer where she had hidden Jesse's bottle—the bottle of water from the spring. In a moment she was back again. The toad still squatted where she had dropped it, the dog still waited at the fence. Winnie pulled out the cork from the mouth of the bottle, and kneeling, she poured the precious water, very slowly and carefully, over the toad.

The dog watched this operation, and then, yawning, he was suddenly bored. He turned and loped away, back down the road to the village. Winnie picked up the toad and held it for a long time, without the least disgust, in the palm of her hand. It sat calmly, blinking, and the water glistened on its back.

The little bottle was empty now. It lay on the grass at Winnie's feet. But if all of it was true, there was more water in the wood. There was plenty more. Just in case. When she was seventeen. If she should decide, there was more water in the wood. Winnie smiled. Then she stooped and put her hand through the fence and set the toad free. "There!" she said. "You're safe. Forever."

Epilogue

THE sign said WELCOME TO TREEGAP, but it was hard to believe that this was really Treegap. The main street hadn't changed so very much, but there were many other streets now, crossing the main street. The road itself was blacktopped. There was a white line painted down its center.

Mae and Tuck, on the seat of a clattering wooden wagon, bumped slowly into Treegap behind the fat old horse. They had seen continuous change and were accustomed to it, but here it seemed shocking and sad. "Look," said Tuck. "Look, Mae. Ain't that where the wood used to be? It's gone! Not a stick or a stump left! And her cottage—that's gone, too."

It was very hard to recognize anything, but from the little hill, which had once lain outside the village and was now very much a part of it, they thought they could figure things out. "Yes," said Mae, "that's where it was, I do believe. 'Course, it's been so long since we was here, I can't tell for certain."

There was a gas station there now. A young man in greasy coveralls was polishing the windshield of a wide and rusty Hudson automobile. As Mae and Tuck rolled past, the young man grinned and said to the driver of the Hudson, who lounged at the wheel, "Looky there. In from the country for a big time." And they chuckled together.

Mae and Tuck clattered on into the village proper, past a catholic mixture of houses which soon gave way to shops and other places of business: a hot-dog stand; a dry cleaner; a pharmacy; a five-and-ten; another gas station; a tall, white frame building with a pleasant verandah, The Treegap Hotel—Family Dining, Easy Rates. The post office. Beyond that, the jailhouse, but a larger jailhouse now, painted brown, with an office for the county clerk. A black and white police car was parked in front, with a red glass searchlight on its roof and a radio antenna, like a buggy whip, fastened to the windshield.

Mae glanced at the jailhouse, but looked away quickly. "See beyond there?" she said, pointing. "That diner? Let's stop there and get a cup of coffee. All right?"

"All right," said Tuck. "Maybe they'll know something."

Inside, the diner gleamed with chrome and smelled like linoleum and ketchup. Mae and Tuck took seats on rumbling swivel stools at the long counter. The counterman emerged from the kitchen at the rear and sized them up expertly. They looked all right. A little queer, maybe—their clothes, especially—but honest. He slapped a cardboard menu down in front of them and leaned on the foaming orangeade cooler. "You folks from off?" he asked.

"Yep," said Tuck. "Just passing through."

"Sure," said the counterman.

"Say," said Tuck cautiously, fingering the menu. "Didn't there used to be a wood once, down the other side of town?"

"Sure," said the counterman. "Had a big electrical storm, though, about three years ago now or thereabouts. Big tree got hit by lightning, split right down the middle. Caught fire and everything. Tore up the ground, too. Had to bulldoze her all out."

"Oh," said Tuck. He and Mae exchanged glances.

"Coffee, please," said Mae. "Black. For both of us."

"Sure," said the counterman. He took the menu away, poured coffee into thick pottery mugs, and leaned again on the orangeade cooler.

"Used to be a fresh-water spring in that wood," said Tuck boldly, sipping his coffee.

"Don't know nothing about that," said the counterman. "Had to bulldoze her all out, like I say."

"Oh," said Tuck.

Afterward, while Mae was shopping for supplies, Tuck went back through the town on foot—back the way they had come—out to the little hill. There were houses there now, and a feed-and-grain store, but on the far side of the hill, inside a rambling iron fence, was a cemetery.

Tuck's heart quickened. He had noticed the cemetery on the way in. Mae had seen it, too. They had not spoken about it. But both knew it might hold other answers. Tuck straightened his old jacket. He passed through an archway of wrought-iron curlicues, and paused, squinting at the weedy rows of grave-stones. And then, far over to the right, he saw a tall monument, once no doubt imposing but now tipped slightly sidewise. On it was carved one name: Foster.

Slowly, Tuck turned his footsteps toward the monument. And saw, as he approached, that there were other, smaller markers all around it. A family plot. And then his throat closed. For it was there. He had wanted it to be there, but now that he saw it, he was overcome with sadness. He knelt and read the inscription:

In Loving Memory
Winifred Foster Jackson
Dear Wife
Dear Mother
1870–1948

"So," said Tuck to himself. "Two years. She's been gone two years." He stood up and looked around, embarrassed, trying to clear the lump from his throat. But there was no one to see him. The cemetery was very quiet. In the branches of a willow behind him, a red-winged blackbird chirped. Tuck wiped his eyes hastily. Then he straightened his jacket again and drew up his hand in a brief salute. "Good girl," he said aloud. And then he turned and left the cemetery, walking quickly.

Later, as he and Mae rolled out of Treegap, Mae said softly, without looking at him, "She's gone?"

Tuck nodded. "She's gone," he answered.

There was a long moment of silence between them, and then Mae said, "Poor Jesse."

"He knowed it, though," said Tuck. "At least, he knowed she wasn't coming. We all knowed that, long time ago."

"Just the same," said Mae. She sighed. And then she sat up a little straighter. "Well, where to now, Tuck? No need to come back here no more."

"That's so," said Tuck. "Let's just head on out this way. We'll locate something."

"All right," said Mae. And then she put a hand on his arm and pointed. "Look out for that toad."

Tuck had seen it, too. He reined in the horse and climbed down from the wagon. The toad was squatting in the middle of the road, quite unconcerned. In the other lane, a pickup truck rattled by, and against the breeze it made, the toad shut its eyes tightly. But it did not move. Tuck waited till the truck had passed, and then he picked up the toad and carried it to the weeds along the road's edge. "Durn fool thing must think it's going to live forever," he said to Mae.

And soon they were rolling on again, leaving Treegap behind, and as they went, the tinkling little melody of a music box drifted out behind them and was lost at last far down the road.

Connected
Readings

from
The Eyes of the Amaryllis

Natalie Babbitt

"WELL, Mother," said the big man uneasily, turning his hat round and round in his hands.

"Well, George," the old woman returned. Her voice was strong and brisk, but, for him, a little critical. She looked up at him from her wing chair by the sunny window and saw—her son, yes, but also a stranger, well into middle age, tall but stooped, with the pale skin and scratchy-looking clothes of an inland man of business. And she saw in him also what he had been: a happy, wild-haired boy running barefoot on the beach. The two were one and the same, no doubt, but she loved the man because she had loved the boy. For her, the boy had been much easier to love.

"So you've broken your ankle," the man said.

"So it seems," she answered. She looked down impatiently at her foot propped up on a hassock. It was thick with bandages and wooden splints, and beside it on the floor a crutch lay waiting. "It's a nuisance, but there you are. Where's my granddaughter? Where's my namesake?"

"She's out on the beach. She's—well, she's never seen the sea before, you know. I suppose she's . . . interested in having a look."

"Interested! Yes, I should imagine so." The old woman smiled faintly.

The man took a deep breath. "Look here, Mother, you know we've always wanted you to come and live with us in Springfield. Now that you're laid up and can't take care of yourself, it's a good time to leave this godforsaken place and come inland where we can look after you."

The old woman shook her head. "It's good of you, George, of course. But when I wrote to you, that wasn't what I had in mind at all. You've brought Geneva down to stay with me, haven't you? That was the plan, wasn't it? My ankle will mend, and when it does, I'll go on the same as I always have."

"I just don't understand it," her son exploded then. "All by yourself here, year after year! The sea pounding, day and night, the dampness, this blasted sand everywhere. And the wind! It never stops! I can hardly bear it for five minutes, and you've been listening to it for thirty years!"

"Fifty, George. You've forgotten. Your father and I, we came here fifty years ago."

"No, but I meant . . ."

"I know what you meant," she said. "You're thinking it's thirty years since the day your father was drowned."

The man gripped his hat more firmly. "All right, Mother, never mind that. Be sensible for once and come back with me. There's plenty of room for three in the buggy, and we can send a wagon later for your things. Surely you can't be so all-fired stubborn about it now, when you can scarcely hobble."

His mother shook her head again. "I don't need you, George. Not yet. It's not time yet. I'll come to you at Christmas, just as I've always done. But the rest of the year I belong right here. Geneva can take care of me till my ankle mends, and then you can come and fetch her."

"But, Mother!"

The old woman frowned at him and her eyes flashed. "George! Enough! We've had this argument a hundred times, and it bores me. You ran away from here a long time ago, and that's all right for you. But I will not budge an inch, not one inch, until . . ." She paused and looked away. Her anger seemed to leave her all at once, and she sighed. "George. Send Geneva in to me and then—go away, George. We only make each other cross."

At this the man seemed to sag a little. A look of pain crossed his face, and he turned half away from her, toward the door, though he watched her still. She was as handsome and vigorous as ever, her gray hair still streaked with red, her back straight as . . . a mast, he thought unwillingly, and then corrected it. Straight as a yardstick. A safer image.

She saw that he was watching her, and her face softened. "George. Dear boy, come and kiss me."

He went to her at once and knelt, and she put her arms around him and pulled him close. For a moment, the last long thirty years dissolved. They were mother and child again, she newly widowed, he newly fatherless, and they clung to each other. Then she loosened her hold and pushed him away gently. "Tell me," she said, smiling at him. "Geneva—what sort of child is she getting to be, do you think?"

"She's exactly like you," he said, sitting back on his heels.

The first Geneva Reade nodded and her eyes twinkled. "It's a judgment on you, George. Well, send her in. And then go home to Springfield and leave me in peace."

The big man kissed his mother's cheek and stood up, putting on his hat. Then, at the door, he said carefully, "I should have thought, though, that you'd want to come away from this spot. I couldn't stand it, looking out there every day, remembering. I'd have gone mad by now."

"Mad?" said his mother. "Well, perhaps I am a little mad."

"Mother," he blurted then, turning back to her, "for the love of heaven, watch out for Jenny. She's all we've got. Don't let her—"

"Hang your clothes on a hickory limb, and don't go near the water," the old woman chanted, bobbing her head from side to side. And then she said, scornfully, "Don't worry. I'll keep her out of the sea. You weren't such a faintheart before your father died."

The man's face closed. "I'll be back in three weeks," he told her flatly. "To fetch Jenny home. And if you're not mended by then, you'll come and stay with us till you are, whether you want to or not."

"Goodbye, George," said his mother, dismissing him. "Have a pleasant ride home. We'll see you in a month or two."

"Three weeks, Mother. Not a moment longer."

"*Goodbye*, George," said the first Geneva Reade.

THE journey that takes a traveler from inland places to the sea will follow roads that stay, in themselves, exactly the same, but they seem to change entirely. Carefree and busy, now leaf-shadowed, now blank and blinding in the summer sunshine, they stretch ahead importantly between green fields, and the air lies lightly on them. But by the time they have come within three miles, then two, then one, of their destination, they have turned submissive. The trees stand back and stand thin, and scrub pines appear, ragged as molting birds. The edges of the roads are lost now in drifts of sand, and the grass, thinner, like the trees, is rough and tall, rising, kneeling, rising, kneeling, as the breeze combs by.

There seems to be more sky here, a great deal more, so that the traveler is made aware, perhaps for the first time, that he moves along quite unprotected on the crust of the earth and might do well to move with caution, lest all at once he fall off, fall up, endlessly, and disappear. So he holds his gaze to the ground and finds that the air has grown heavy with new, wet smells, and the roads and everything around them look uncared-for. But this is not the case. They are cared for with the closest attention—by the sea.

The second Geneva Reade had observed all this on the way to

Gran's house and was astonished by it in spite of the heavy presence beside her in the buggy. Her father had not spoken a word for miles, and he had allowed the horse to slow its pace to a clopping walk. His clenched hands, wrapped in the reins, were white at the knuckles. Jenny observed this, also, but she could not worry about it now. She was going to see the ocean for the first time in her life.

To be away from home—to stay with Gran and help her while her ankle mended—this seemed a very grownup thing to do, and Jenny had boasted about it to her friends. But in truth she was a little alarmed about that part, though her grandmother, whom she had seen before only for the two weeks of the yearly Christmas season, had long been a figure of romance to her. Gran was not like other grandmothers, smelling of starch or mothballs, depending on the time of year, and spending their time watering their plants. Gran stood straight and proud. Her face and arms were sunburned. And though she talked and listened, there always seemed to be something else on her mind, something far more absorbing than Christmas conversation.

But Jenny did not care for household chores, and was not at all sure that somewhere in her lay hidden the makings of a bedside nurse. So it wasn't that part of her adventure that excited her. No, the real enticement was the ocean. But this she could not admit. She was the only one of her friends who had never been to the shore. Preposterous, when it was only thirty miles from Springfield! But her father had never let her come, had always refused to discuss it. He hardly ever went, himself, to see Gran at her house.

But now, because of Gran's ankle, all that had changed. She was going to see the ocean, and she had all she could do to keep from bouncing on the buggy's padded seat. When would the water show itself? Over the next rise? Now! The buggy started up—and then she had gasped once and sat erect and very still.

For there it was, suddenly, the great Atlantic, so vast a thing that all of her imaginings could never have prepared her. It stretched away so far beyond the grassy plain that its sharp horizon curved to prove the roundness of the planet. In an instant she felt diminished, and with that new sensation came an unexpected sense of freedom. The breath she had caught and held slipped out in a long sigh, and she turned her head to see how her father was responding to the sight. But his face was rigid as a stone.

So she had turned back, and as the buggy rolled nearer, the coastline below them revealed itself slowly. A bay emerged and, far to the leftward tilt of its concavity, a tidy-looking town, with docks and the hulls of a few small ships. Then, as the buggy, reaching a fork, turned right, she saw that there were houses scattered all along the shore. Far to the right, however, they sat fewer and farther between until at last there was only one house, quite by itself, on a low bluff at the farthest edge of the bay, where the land curved slowly in and down and sank a heavy arm into the water.

"Is that Gran's house?" she had asked, pointing.

"Yes," said her father.

"That's where you lived when you were little?"

"Yes," he said shortly.

Her head filled at once with a thousand questions, but it was clear that he didn't want to talk. "I can ask Gran," she had thought to herself. "Later."

When the buggy rolled down and stopped at last beside the house, Jenny had climbed out slowly, her eyes turned to the beach. "Can I go and look?" she pleaded. "Before I go in to see Gran?"

"All right, I guess so," her father said. "But, Jenny, remember what I told you. Stay back from the water. Don't ever forget that it's dangerous." And then, taking down her satchel, he had gone to the door of the house, knocked once, and stepped inside.

The sea did not look dangerous. Jenny saw the whole of its low-tide shore behavior in one long glance—how it tipped and slopped, sifting the wet sand, stroking the beach with sliding foam. Well up on this beach, a straggling fringe of seaweed, like a scratchy penline, lay drying where the last high tide had stranded it, and here, too, intermingled, had been left abandoned pebbles by the million and broken bits of shell. Above the seaweed the toast-colored sand was loose and warm, and she longed to take off her shoes and stockings and dig her toes into it. Not now. Later. After her father had gone. Gran had promised her that if she, Jenny, were ever allowed to visit here, there would be much to do on the beach, things that could only be done correctly if one were barefoot.

Jenny took a cautious step over the seaweed line, down to where the sand was hard and wet, and at once a sly finger of foam slid up and curled around her ankle. She leapt back and the foam slipped away with a sigh, to be lost beneath the curl of the next small wave. Now new fingers of foam reached for her up the sand, and she retreated behind the seaweed reluctantly. Another wave, a soft thump, the slide of foam, repeated over and over again. She watched it, amazed and faintly hypnotized, and the feeling of freedom that had come to her at first grew deeper. Wisps of her dark red hair, tied back so neatly at home by her mother, blew about her face as the breeze swept past her, and suddenly it seemed as if she could hear it speaking. *True to yo-o-o-ou*, it whispered, and the foam answered: *Yes-s-s* (thump) *yes-s-s* (thump) *yes-s-s.*

"Jenny!"

She heard her father's voice behind her and, turning, plodded up across the sand to where he stood at the edge of the swaying grass.

"Jenny, look at you. You've soaked one foot already," he said despairingly. "Will you promise to stay safe, now? Will you be careful? I've kept you away from this place as long as I could, and—I know you're nearly grown, but still, it worries me to death to leave you here."

"I'll be careful, Papa," she said.

He put his hands on her shoulders and peered into her face, and then, dropping his hands, he shrugged. "Well, do your best to be useful to your grandmother. It's remarkable how she never seems to change, but still, she's getting on. You'll see. She's waiting for you—better go on in. I'll be back in three weeks."

"All right, Papa."

He left her, then, and climbed into the buggy, and as he urged the horse into a turn, she saw the stiffness of his shoulders ease, and he looked back at her almost cheerfully. "Goodbye!" he called.

She answered, "Goodbye," and added, to herself, "He's happy to be leaving." She watched him go and felt stranded and lonely, like the pebbles, but then she turned back for one more look at the sea and the lonely feeling fled away. For it seemed as if she had known this beach and loved it all her life, that she belonged here; that coming to this place, with its endless sky and water, was a kind of coming home.

The Time Traveler

Matt Bai

JOHNSON space center, a rolling campus about a half hour from downtown Houston, is awash in history. The giant Apollo rockets lie like fallen monuments at the entrance; inside, the original mission-control room ("Houston, we have a problem") is preserved as a shrine. In the spring of 1998, one of NASA's most prized relics, 77-year-old John Glenn, took his friend Bill Clinton on a tour of the cavernous hangar known as Building Nine. On the mid-deck of the space-shuttle simulator, Glenn and his guest wolfed down some rehydrated mushrooms and beans. With Clinton still nursing an injured knee, nervous Secret Service agents said he couldn't go up to the flight deck. "Oh, I'll ask him," Glenn said mischievously, and soon he and the president were climbing the narrow ladder to the cockpit, like kids in a treehouse.

For Glenn, however, the fun soon gave way to hours spent studying training manuals. He would be a human test subject on Discovery, giving blood and urine, plastering himself with electrodes to measure his heart rate. He would swallow a pill the size of a bottle cap, inside of which was a tiny thermometer and transmitter to gauge his body temperature. He would be learning to sleep, shower and share space in zero gravity for nine days. On his first historic flight, 36 years ago, Glenn had been strapped into the Friendship 7 capsule alone, barely able to move, much less float around. When it came to flying the shuttle—the most complicated vehicle ever built, with more than 800 control switches, 2,600 cargo items, 83 scientific experiments and a satellite on board—the old man had a lot to learn.

So began the re-education of the world's oldest astronaut for his final mission, which begins when Discovery blasts off from Cape Canaveral. At times, exhausted by 12-hour days in the classrooms and simulators at Johnson, Glenn seemed like a grandfather trying to program his VCR. "Yup . . . yup . . . yup," he repeated, squinting through glasses and nodding slowly. But NASA's crack instructors soon found out what anyone who knew the longtime senator could have told them: Glenn doesn't always get things right the first time, but he's simply unable to give up. Day after day, he attacked the most tedious assignments—learning to use a 70-mm camera or a blood centrifuge—for hours on end without a hint of frustration. This was the John Glenn from the Mercury days, the "clean Marine" who ran laps at Langley Air Force Base while his fellow astronauts slept in. After all these years, he was still the John Glenn of American lore—the Midwestern hero who convinced us, through doggedness and decency, that American ingenuity would ultimately win the day.

Back then, Glenn's mission seemed to be a question of survival. Now that we've come through the cold war, the issue is how to live longer, and better. Weightlessness seems to age the body, and scientists wonder if there may be a connection between gravity and getting older that might someday help them offset the aging process. They have no idea what they'll find by studying Glenn, but all science begins with simple observation. And as 75 million Americans hurtle toward old age, it's nice to be reminded that a grandfather—even if he isn't your average grandfather—can do a lot more than crossword puzzles.

It's not at all clear that sending Glenn into space will change humankind. Since space travelers and the elderly suffer from some of the same maladies (muscle and bone loss, sleep disruption, loss of balance), studying astronauts is like watching the aging process in fast-forward. So observing an old person outside Earth's atmosphere could yield more clues about the symptoms of old age—and whether they're reversible. The most important of Glenn's 12 experiments will measure his sleep patterns and the rate at which his body breaks down proteins. The senator couldn't be more pumped; he's talked more about urine samples in the last six months than any politician on record.

NASA's younger generation has always viewed Glenn with reverence—and a hint of sympathy. He was arguably the world's most famous astronaut, but he was also the guy who got shafted. Denied another flight after his four-hour trip in 1962, he had to watch those who came after him walk on the moon. Glenn never stopped dreaming of that second chance. "It'll probably never happen," he once confided to his daughter, Lynn. NASA's decision in January to finally put Glenn back in a spacesuit made for a happy ending, but was sure to ignite debate. Former astronauts grumbled that Glenn was staging the world's most expensive publicity stunt. Clinton's aides, meanwhile, worried that Glenn's flight would seem like payback for a loyal Democrat.

Glenn had more important critics to worry about: his wife, Annie, and their two children. Questioned about Annie's feelings, Glenn liked to say she was "cool" to the idea. In fact, she was just about frozen. After 55 years of enduring her husband's adventures—including the moment in 1962 when his heat shield burned up on re-entry—Annie couldn't wait for Glenn's retirement from the Senate. "I was looking forward to getting John back for my own," she told NEWSWEEK. "I had given him to our government ever since we'd been married. I was a little jealous."

Glenn's two children—53-year-old David, a doctor, and 52-year-old Lynn, a social worker—were even less enthusiastic. "I don't want this for you, and I don't want this for the rest of us," Lynn told him bluntly. At a dinner in Washington, Glenn introduced David to NASA Administrator Dan Goldin. "Well, you must be excited," Goldin said. "Actually, no," David replied evenly. "I'm entirely against it." An embarrassed Glenn told Goldin, "I'll take care of this."

Glenn brought Annie to his classes and showed her the toiletries and outfits he had selected from NASA's stockpile: size-10 slippers, size-36 briefs, three handkerchiefs ("I might get the sniffles up there"), a Swiss Army knife and bulky diapers for the long wait before liftoff. Seeing her husband so thrilled changed Annie's mind. Her children, weary from a childhood spent worrying that their father could die at any moment, were harder to convince. "Do I want him to do it? No," Lynn says. "Would I ask him not to do it? Never. This is who he is."

Glenn had always been angry that NASA wouldn't let his kids see the Friendship 7 capsule on the launch pad. "I thought that Daddy was going to be off on a brand-new experience," he says, "and I wanted them to have the same kind of confidence that I had that I was coming back." So this time he took his grandsons, 16-year-old Daniel and 13-year-old Zach, to Johnson and showed them around the shuttle mock-up. "Grandpa, you're crazy to go up in this thing," one of them gasped. Later, Annie asked Zach if he felt better about the flight. "Grandma, I'm scared," he told her. "Well, I am, too," she said with a sigh. "That's normal."

From the beginning, Glenn insisted that everyone at NASA call him "John," not "Senator." But he could never be just another astronaut. Traveling alone on his first trip to Johnson, he was mobbed by well-wishers as he tried to change planes in St. Louis. In the NASA cafeteria, so many staffers wanted to wish him luck that he could hardly find time to eat. Glenn never failed to shake a hand or sign an autograph. "I thought he'd be a typical politician," said one instructor. "But now I think he's just the nicest grandpa you could ever have."

Glenn arrived at Johnson as early as 7 A.M., ready for a grueling day of lectures. He shared an office two thirds the size of his Senate digs with his six fellow astronauts. There, Glenn regaled the crew with stories of the early days and dismissed the movie version of "The Right Stuff" with a wave of his hand. "That's not how it was," he said. "I'll *tell* you how it was." He told them that the only time he had ever felt sick in the capsule was when he was bobbing in the ocean, waiting to be rescued. And NASA's Friendship 7 patch was a fraud, Glenn complained, because he hadn't worn a patch.

Glenn spoke frequently with some of his old Mercury colleagues. In July he told Alan Shepard that he would arrange for Shepard's daughter to attend the launch. He wanted Shepard to come, too, but his old friend and rival declined, saying it was more than he could do. He died of leukemia a few weeks later. (His widow, one of Annie's closest friends, died shortly after.) Glenn felt as if he'd lost a brother. He and the other three remaining Mercury astronauts attended an emotional service at Johnson before Glenn, the oldest of them, went back to work.

It helped that Glenn was in remarkable physical shape. He's careful to eat light and healthy—usually just fruit or soup for lunch—and he power-walks near his suburban Maryland home. (His only vice is chocolate; Glenn was thrilled to see that the shuttle has a junk-food drawer.) When Glenn had to remove his shirt and attach electrodes to his chest to practice for monitoring his heart rate, a TV crew offered to leave the room. "Doesn't bother me," Glenn said with a shrug—then happily pointed out his scars from small incisions made on his torso during his Mercury training.

Not everyone was amused by Glenn's ease with the media. The shuttle commander, Curt Brown, objected when NASA wanted to wire the crew with TV microphones during training. Although the 42-year-old Brown admired Glenn, he worried about a tightly packed mission, and there were days when he wondered why he wanted to lead what the media called "the Glenn flight." His mother—a huge Glenn fan—brought him back to Earth. "You have to remember what you're doing here and who you're flying with," she scolded.

What did bother Glenn was the charge that science was just a lame excuse to shoot him back into space. One morning in June, Glenn delighted photographers by wearing the bizarre-looking harness of electrodes that he would wear on his head while sleeping during flight. But later, he interrupted his classroom work to put the photographers on notice. "We have to talk about those pictures this morning," he snapped, jabbing a forefinger into the air. "I am very serious about this. If you use them to demonstrate the science involved, OK. But if you use those photos to ridicule, then we'll cut off all access to you." It was as close to losing his cool as John Glenn gets.

Back in Washington, Glenn was also trying to wind down a 24-year Senate career. "I've got two jobs—that's my problem," he said, only half kidding. As the buzzer signaling a pending vote went off in his office, Glenn cut short an interview and called for an aide to brief him. "It's [Lauch] Faircloth," Glenn said, referring to his Republican rival from North Carolina, as he squinted at the closed-circuit TV. "I'm probably against it." On his way to the Senate floor, Glenn shared the elevator with Louisiana Democrat John Breaux. "We're all going down to the launch. We're very proud," Breaux chirped. "Of course, we'll have to hold a caucus to see whether we want him to come back down."

Even some of Glenn's colleagues wonder: how can anyone so famous remain so ordinary? To answer the question, it helps to get on Route 70 in Columbus, Ohio, and drive east for about an hour to New Concord, population 2,000. Glenn still owns his boyhood home here, a white house shaded by maple trees on the street now known as Friendship Drive. The Presbyterian settlers of New Concord didn't drink, smoke or play cards. Glenn's favorite playmate was Annie Castor, a girl down the street who stuttered so severely that she couldn't speak in class. "I knew exactly what kind of person she was, so I married her," Glenn says. He and Annie now fly his twin-prop between D.C. and Ohio. They like to show up at the John Glenn High School football games, or at Tom's Ice Cream Bowl in Zanesville, where a cheeseburger costs $1.80 and the hot-fudge sundaes still come in soup bowls.

If it's true, as Annie says, that her husband has nine lives, then he's used a few of them by now—in World War II and Korea, as a test pilot and a spaceman. The last was his defining moment. The Russian Yuri Gagarin's first-ever orbital flight in April 1961 stunned the West, and someone had to match it. On Feb. 20, 1962, Glenn made history, lifting off to those chilling words: "Godspeed, John Glenn." But NASA refused to let him fly again; John Kennedy thought him too much of an icon to be placed atop another explosive rocket.

Disappointed, Glenn wandered out into the world of politics. He ran for president in 1984, but the campaign crashed and burned, leaving him with debts he's still paying down. One day during the campaign, on the way to work with her father, Lynn Glenn was surprised to find him driving instead to the Smithsonian Air and Space Museum, where the Friendship 7 capsule is housed. He strolled the halls while she waited in the car. "Do you come here often?" Lynn asked him when he returned. In a rare reflective moment, Glenn said he sometimes needed to remember how he and his NASA colleagues had toiled so hard and risked so much for a common goal. Politics just wasn't the same.

But as Glenn prepares to go into quarantine with the rest of the shuttle crew, he's left the rancor behind. His only fear now is that he'll somehow fumble his tests in space. What if he can't sleep in the harness the way he did in Harvard's sleep lab in Boston? What if his veins can't be tapped for 12 blood samples? (Glenn hates "getting stuck," and drawing blood in zero gravity can take almost an hour.) "Don't pray for my safety," Glenn told a college pal. "If you're going to pray for me, pray that I do well."

When the mission is over, Glenn will pack up his life's mementos and ship them off to Ohio State University, which is building a $20 million institute in his name. There are plans to turn his childhood home into a museum. And when at last his remarkable American odyssey is over, John Glenn will rest in Arlington National Cemetery among the heroes of the republic. How would he like to be remembered? "This may sound strange, but I've never really sat back and thought about it," Glenn says. "I'm not done yet." Whatever Glenn's flight tells scientists about aging, he's already shown the rest of us how to grow old.

Peekaboo, I Almost See You

Ogden Nash

Middle-aged life is merry, and I love to lead it,
But there comes a day when your eyes are all right but your
    arm isn't long enough to hold the telephone book where
    you can read it,
And your friends get jocular, so you go to the oculist,
And of all your friends he is the joculist,
So over his facetiousness let us skim,
Only noting that he has been waiting for you ever since you said
    Good evening to his grandfather clock under the impres-
    sion that it was him,
And you look at his chart and it says SHRDLU QWERTYOP,
    and you say Well, why SHRDNTLU QWERTYOP? and he
    says one set of glasses won't do.
You need two,
One for reading Erle Stanley Gardner's Perry Mason and
    Keats's "Endymion" with,
And the other for walking around without saying Hello to
    strange wymion with.
So you spend your time taking off your seeing glasses to put
    on your reading glasses, and then remembering that your
    reading glasses are upstairs or in the car,
And then you can't find your seeing glasses again because
    without them you can't see where they are.
Enough of such mishaps, they would try the patience of an
    ox,
I prefer to forget both pairs of glasses and pass my declining
    years saluting strange women and grandfather clocks.

from
Virtual Reality: A Door to Cyberspace

Ann E. Weiss

Chapter 1: To Change the World?

REALITY must sometimes feel grim to Christopher Cobbs of Grants Pass, Oregon. Christopher was born with cerebral palsy. Cerebral palsy is a disorder that interferes with the ability to control muscle movement. Christopher will probably never walk on his own.

But for Christopher, the prospect of life in a wheelchair is only one kind of reality. On a day in 1994, he experienced a different kind.

In this other reality, Christopher propelled himself across grassy lawns and splashed through puddles—without venturing outdoors. He crossed busy streets and skidded over icy pavements, never noticing that he lacked mittens and boots. In this reality, Christopher maneuvered his wheelchair through the classrooms and corridors of a grade school he had never actually entered. In fact, the school does not even exist in what most of us call "reality."

The more Christopher explored, the more fantastic his new reality seemed. Orderly neighborhoods of houses, sidewalks, and shrubs sprouted colorful twisting pyramids. Ball-shaped objects spiraled across streets. Weird sculptures flashed into sight, only to vanish mysteriously. Suddenly, Christopher felt himself teetering on the very edge of earth itself. Taking a deep breath and clutching the joystick firmly, he leaned forward, swooping and soaring into the bright blue void beyond.

Then it was over. The void faded as someone switched off the computer at Christopher's side. Someone else removed the headset through which Christopher had viewed the trees and houses, the whirling shapes, and the deep void of the strange world he had left behind. The boy took his hand from the joystick he had used to control his movements in that world. His wheelchair stopped moving. The system of rollers under the wheelchair stopped, too. That system had been designed to reproduce the feeling of bumping over grass, slipping on ice, and leaving firm ground to soar into space. Christopher was back in his own reality. He was back in the world as we know it.

Where had he been a moment before? What sort of reality had he visited? Different people have different names for it, but the one we hear most often is virtual reality—VR, for short.

What Is Virtual Reality?

Many who have experienced VR say it is a form of reality startlingly like our own. The word *virtual* means "being so in effect, though not in name or according to strict definition." Virtual reality is not the actual physical reality of everyday life. Yet sometimes it seems to come close.

That is not to say that virtually real worlds are always realistic. Houses in the neighborhood Christopher Cobbs toured looked more like cartoon drawings than real-life dwellings, for example. As we will see, VR technology is not yet sophisticated enough to permit most virtual objects to look entirely lifelike. And spiraling colors and blue voids are not a part of everyday reality. The scientists who created Christopher's virtual world added those fantasy elements just for fun.

Yet despite the unreal quality of some virtual scenes, VR's overall you-are-there effect can be compelling. A reporter for *Business Week* magazine described a virtual battlefield scene used to train U.S. soldiers. She admitted to ducking in fear as the tanks roared toward her. Shells seemed to explode in her face. Soldiers watching similar scenes break into sweat and start swearing, she noted. That is exactly what they would do during a real-life battle. A California girl briefly confused the virtual world and the real one after playing a VR video game. "Which way was I facing?" she asked, taking off her headset. "You feel like you're there," the girl said of the virtual world.

Howard Rheingold agrees. Rheingold is a writer who has visited many virtual environments. In one, he used a virtual fishing rod to hook a virtual fish. "I did feel a sensation spookily similar to that feeling of something *alive* at the other end of the line," Rheingold says.

But although people may agree as to what virtual reality is

like, they tend to argue about exactly what it *is.* So far, no one has come up with a single, strict definition of VR.

There's some agreement, of course. Everyone starts with the fact that VR is an experience created by means of a computer. The computer is fed a huge amount of information. A human programmer loads the computer with facts and figures about the layout of a typical grade school, for example, or the rules of a video game. Then the computer processes that information. It transforms facts and figures into images that look, move, and behave much as if they were actual objects that truly existed in the real world. If the computer-generated images are convincing enough, people who see them will feel that they have left ordinary reality behind. They will have the impression that they have plunged into—become immersed in—a new reality. *Immersion* is a key word in defining VR.

Interactive is another. Not only do people who use VR feel that they are immersed in a virtual environment, they feel that they are acting and doing things in that environment. Christopher Cobbs used a joystick to tell the computer which way he wanted his wheelchair to travel through the virtual neighborhood. The computer responded to him by displaying a scene that changed continuously as he rolled down the street. At the same time, the computer instructed the mechanisms under Christopher's wheelchair how to move. The mechanisms reproduced the sensations of rolling along sidewalks and swerving around obstacles. In other VR setups, users wear computerized gloves, vests, or suits that cover most of the body. Such devices allow them to feel that they are touching objects in the virtual world, even moving those objects around.

Beyond "interaction" and "immersion," however, agreement about the nature of virtual reality begins to fall apart. How lifelike does an experience have to be to be considered virtually real? Opinions differ. Do video games count as VR? More differences of opinion. What kind of equipment—and how much of it—is needed to enter a virtual world? Is a home computer enough? Or do you need a headset, glove, and other elaborate devices? Will it ever be possible to have a virtual experience with no special equipment at all? The arguments continue.

On one subject, though, most people agree: VR is a bold new technology with exciting possibilities for the future. "Properly done," says David Bonini, head of one company that produces VR technology, "virtual reality has an opportunity to change the world."

Using VR

Virtual reality has already changed Christopher Cobbs's world. Thanks to VR, Christopher found out what it is like to operate a wheelchair over different kinds of surfaces: grassy, muddy, hard, and ice covered. He learned how to move safely through a neighborhood like the one he lives in. He practiced getting around inside a school. He turned corners, used the water cooler, and did much more. Christopher's experiences in virtual reality should make his real life a little easier.

What is more, the change VR has made in Christopher's life may help bring about changes in the lives of other disabled people. Christopher's introduction to VR came at the Oregon Research Institute in Eugene, Oregon. Scientists there were trying to find out whether VR can help youngsters in wheelchairs cut the amount of time they need to learn to use them in real-life situations. Christopher's experience suggests that it can.

VR may help the disabled in other ways. In a Chicago project called Wheelchair VR, an architect's plans for a new hospital were fed into a computer. The computer turned the plans into a virtual hospital as real-seeming as Christopher Cobbs's virtual school. Now, although the hospital was still unbuilt and actually existed only on paper, its planners could "see" it. They could even "enter" it, just as Christopher entered his school. Pretending to be real-life patients in wheelchairs, they "explored" the virtual hospital. They turned virtual lights on and off. They opened virtual windows and navigated virtual hallways. In the process, they made a dismaying discovery. Seated in their virtual wheelchairs, the planners could not reach any of the virtual sink faucets! The sinks were changed—made wheelchair accessible—*before* the hospital was built. Virtual reality had helped correct a serious design flaw.

The disabled are not the only ones who may benefit from VR. Consider some other ongoing projects:

• In North Carolina, medical researchers are using VR to conduct experiments involving microscopic bits of matter called molecules. Real-life molecules are too small to be seen with the naked eye. The virtual models, however, appear to measure two feet across. Reaching their gloved hands into the virtual world, the researchers try fitting the models together. Each virtual fit may be a clue as to how real molecules form combinations. The researchers hope that some of the molecular patterns they discover in VR will help them develop actual lifesaving medicines.

• In Connecticut, a student doctor performs her first operation. She has little experience, so mistakes are possible. If she does make a mistake, though, no real harm will be done. The student is operating on an indestructible virtual patient, not a living human being.

• Near Washington, D.C., U.S. Army doctors are working on a way to treat wounded soldiers by means of VR. They hope to develop special VR robots that will enable them to perform operations on men and women stranded on the battlefield—while the doctors themselves are miles away.

• Across the country, in Washington State, aircraft mechanics at the Boeing Company are using VR to "repair" virtual engines. The actual engines are still in the planning stage. Like the Wheelchair VR architects in Chicago, these mechanics are looking for possible design problems. If they find problems, they will correct them. Routine maintenance and repairs on actual engines will be more convenient—and cheaper. In the mid-1990s, Boeing engineers were designing the company's new 777 model plane entirely by computer.

• Across the Pacific Ocean, a Japanese company has placed an order for a robot to be operated through VR technology. Plans call for the robot to be capable of spray painting skyscraper-sized buildings anywhere on earth.

A robot that can go anywhere and paint anything? Long-distance surgery? Gigantic virtual molecules? No wonder David Bonini predicts that VR will change the world. But change it how?

The Happiness Machine

Ray Bradbury

ON Sunday morning Leo Auffmann moved slowly through his garage, expecting some wood, a curl of wire, a hammer or wrench to leap up crying, "Start here!" But nothing leaped, nothing cried for a beginning.

Should a Happiness Machine, he wondered, be something you can carry in your pocket?

Or, he went on, should it be something that carries you in *its* pocket?

"One thing I absolutely *know*," he said aloud. "It should be *bright!*"

He set a can of orange paint in the center of the workbench, picked up a dictionary, and wandered into the house.

"Lena?" He glanced at the dictionary. "Are you 'pleased, contented, joyful, delighted'? Do you feel 'lucky, fortunate'? Are things 'clever and fitting,' 'successful and suitable' for you?"

Lena stopped slicing vegetables and closed her eyes. "Read me the list again, please," she said.

He shut the book.

"What have I done, you got to stop and think an hour before you can tell me? All I ask is a simple yes or no! You're *not* contented, delighted, joyful?"

"Cows are 'contented,' babies and old people in second childhood are 'delighted,' God help them," she said. "As for 'joyful,' Leo? Look how I laugh scrubbing out the sink. . . ."

He peered closely at her and his face relaxed. "Lena, it's true. A man doesn't appreciate. Next month, maybe, we'll get away."

"*I'm* not complaining!" she cried. "*I'm* not the one comes in with a list saying, 'Stick out your tongue.' Leo, do you ask what makes your heart beat all night? No! Next will you ask, 'What's marriage?' Who knows, Leo? Don't ask. A man who thinks like that, how it runs, how things work, falls off the trapeze in the circus, chokes wondering how the muscles work in the throat. Eat, sleep, breathe, Leo, and stop staring at me like I'm something new in the house!"

Lena Auffmann froze. She sniffed the air.

"Oh, my God, look what you done!"

She yanked the oven door open. A great cloud of smoke poured through the kitchen.

"Happiness!" she wailed. "And for the first time in six months we have a fight! Happiness, and for the first time in twenty years it's not bread, it's charcoal for supper!"

When the smoke cleared, Leo Auffmann was gone.

The fearful clangor, the collision of man and inspiration, the flinging about of metal, lumber, hammer, nails, T square, screwdriver, continued for many days. On occasion, defeated, Leo Auffmann loitered out through the streets, nervous, apprehensive, jerking his head at the slightest sound of distant laughter, listened to children's jokes, watching what made them smile. At night he sat on neighbors' crowded porches, listening to the old folks weigh and balance life, and at each explosion of merriment Leo Auffmann quickened like a general who has seen the forces of darkness routed and whose strategy has been reaffirmed. On his way home he felt triumphant until he was in his garage with the dead tools and the inanimate lumber. Then his bright face fell away in a pale funk, and to cover his sense of failure he banged and crashed the parts of his machine about as if they really did make sense. At last it began to shape itself and at the end of ten days and nights, trembling with fatigue, self-dedicated, half starved, fumbling and looking as if he had been riven by lightning, Leo Auffmann wandered into his house.

The children, who had been screaming horribly at each other, fell silent, as if the Red Death had entered at the chiming of the clock.

"The Happiness Machine," husked Leo Auffmann, "is ready."

"Leo Auffmann," said his wife, "has lost fifteen pounds. He hasn't talked to his children in two weeks, they are nervous, they fight, listen! His wife is nervous, she's gained ten pounds, she'll need new clothes, look! Sure—the machine is ready. But happy? Who can say? Leo, leave off with the clock you're building. You'll never find a cuckoo big enough to go in it! Man was not made to tamper with such things. It's not against God, no, but it sure looks like it's against Leo Auffmann. Another week of this and we'll bury him in his machine!"

But Leo Auffmann was too busy noticing that the room was falling swiftly up.

How interesting, he thought, lying on the floor.

Darkness closed in a great wink on him as someone screamed something about that Happiness Machine, three times.

The first thing he noticed the next morning was dozens of birds fluttering around in the air stirring up ripples like colored stones thrown into an incredibly clear stream, gonging the tin roof of the garage softly.

A pack of multibred dogs pawfooted one by one into the yard to peer and whine gently through the garage door; four boys, two girls, and some men hesitated in the driveway and then edged along under the cherry trees.

Leo Auffmann, listening, knew what it was that had reached out and called them all into the yard.

The sound of the Happiness Machine.

It was the sort of sound that might be heard coming from a giant's kitchen on a summer day. There were all kinds of hummings, low and high, steady and then changing. Incredible foods were being baked there by a host of whirring golden bees as big as teacups. The giantess herself, humming contentedly under her breath, might glide to the door, as vast as all summer, her face a huge peach-colored moon gazing calmly out upon smiling dogs, corn-haired boys and flour-haired old men.

"Wait," said Leo Auffmann out loud. "I didn't turn the machine on this morning! Saul!"

Saul, standing in the yard below, looked up.

"Saul, did you turn it on?"

"You told me to warm it up half an hour ago!"

"All right, Saul, I forgot. I'm not awake." He fell back in bed.

His wife, bringing his breakfast up, paused by the window, looking down at the garage.

"Tell me," she said quietly. "If that machine is like you say, has it got an answer to making babies in it somewhere? Can that machine make seventy-year-old people twenty? Also, how does death look when you hide in there with all that happiness?"

"Hide!"

"If you died from overwork, what should I do today, climb in that big box down there and be happy? Also tell me, Leo, how is our life? You know how our house is. Seven in the morning, breakfast, the kids; all of you gone by eight-thirty and it's just me and washing and me and cooking and socks to be darned, weeds to be dug, or I run to the store or polish silver. Who's complaining? I'm just reminding you how the house is put together, Leo, what's in it! So now answer: How do you get all those things I said in one machine?"

"That's not how it's built!"

"I'm sorry. I got no time to look, then."

And she kissed his cheek and went from the room and he lay smelling the wind that blew from the hidden machine below, rich with the odor of those roasted chestnuts that are sold in the autumn streets of a Paris he had never known. . . .

A cat moved unseen among the hypnotized dogs and boys to purr against the garage door, in the sound of snow-waves crumbling down a faraway and rhythmically breathing shore.

Tomorrow, thought Leo Auffmann, we'll try the machine, all of us, together.

Late that night he awoke and knew something had wakened him. Far away in another room he heard someone crying.

"Saul?" he whispered, getting out of bed.

In his room Saul wept, his head buried in his pillow. "No . . . no . . ." he sobbed. "Over . . . over . . ."

"Saul, you had a nightmare? Tell me about it, son."

But the boy only wept.

And sitting there on the boy's bed, Leo Auffmann suddenly thought to look out the window. Below, the garage doors stood open.

He felt the hairs rise along the back of his neck.

When Saul slept again, uneasily, whimpering, his father went downstairs and out to the garage where, not breathing, he put his hand out.

In the cool night the Happiness Machine's metal was too hot to touch.

So, he thought, Saul was here tonight.

Why? Was Saul unhappy, in need of the machine? No, happy, but wanting to hold on to happiness always. Could you blame a boy wise enough to know his position who tried to keep it that way? No! And yet . . .

Above, quite suddenly, something white was exhaled from Saul's window. Leo Auffmann's heart thundered. Then he realized the window curtain had blown out into the open night. But it had seemed as intimate and shimmering a thing as a boy's soul escaping his room. And Leo Auffmann had flung up his hands as if to thwart it, push it back into the sleeping house.

Cold, shivering, he moved back into the house and up to Saul's room where he seized the blowing curtain in and locked the window tight so the pale thing could not escape again. Then he sat on the bed and put his hand on Saul's back.

"*A Tale of Two Cities?* Mine. *The Old Curiosity Shop?* Ha, that's Leo Auffmann's all right! *Great Expectations?* That *used* to be mine. But let *Great Expectations* be his, now!"

"What's this?" asked Leo Auffmann, entering.

"This," said his wife, "is sorting out the community property! When a father scares his son at night it's time to chop everything in half! Out of the way, Mr. Bleak House, Old Curiosity Shop. In all these books, no mad scientist lives like Leo Auffmann, none!"

"You're leaving, and you haven't even tried the machine!" he protested. "Try it once, you'll unpack, you'll stay!"

"*Tom Swift and His Electric Annihilator*—whose is that?" she asked. "Must I *guess?*"

Snorting, she gave *Tom Swift* to Leo Auffmann.

Very late in the day all the books, dishes, clothes, linens had been stacked one here, one there, four here, four there, ten here, ten there. Lena Auffmann, dizzy with counting, had to sit down. "All right," she gasped. "Before I go, Leo, prove you don't give nightmares to innocent sons!"

Silently Leo Auffmann led his wife into the twilight. She stood before the eight-foot-tall, orange-colored box.

"That's *happiness?*" she said. "Which button do I press to be overjoyed, grateful, contented, and much-obliged?"

The children had gathered now.

"Mama," said Saul, "don't!"

"I got to know what I'm yelling about, Saul." She got in the machine, sat down, and looked out at her husband, shaking her head. "It's not me needs this, it's you, a nervous wreck, shouting."

"Please," he said, "you'll see!"

He shut the door.

"Press the button!" he shouted in at his unseen wife.

There was a click. The machine shivered quietly, like a huge dog dreaming in its sleep.

"Papa!" said Saul, worried.

"Listen!" said Leo Auffmann.

At first there was nothing but the tremor of the machine's own secretly moving cogs and wheels.

"Is Mama all right?" asked Naomi.

"All right? She's fine! There, now . . . there!"

And inside the machine Lena Auffmann could be heard saying, "Oh!" and then again, "Ah!" in a startled voice. "Look at that!" said his hidden wife. "Paris!" and later, "London! There goes Rome! The Pyramids! The Sphinx!"

"The Sphinx, you hear, children?" Leo Auffmann whispered and laughed.

"Perfume!" cried Lena Auffmann, surprised.

Somewhere a phonograph played "The Blue Danube" faintly.

"Music! I'm dancing!"

"Only *thinks* she's dancing," the father confided to the world.

"Amazing!" said the unseen woman.

Leo Auffmann blushed. "What an understanding wife."

And then inside the Happiness Machine, Lena Auffmann began to weep.

The inventor's smile faded.

"She's crying," said Naomi.

"She can't be!"

"She is," said Saul.

"She simply can't be crying!" Leo Auffmann, blinking, pressed his ear to the machine. "But . . . yes . . . like a baby . . ."

He could only open the door.

"Wait." There his wife sat, tears rolling down her cheeks. "Let me finish." She cried some more.

Leo Auffmann turned off the machine, stunned.

"Oh, it's the saddest thing in the world!" she wailed. "I feel awful, terrible." She climbed out through the door. "First, there was Paris . . ."

"What's wrong with Paris?"

"I never even *thought* of being in Paris in my life. But now you got me thinking: Paris! So suddenly I want to be in Paris and I know I'm not!"

"It's almost as good, this machine."

"No. Sitting in there, I knew. I thought, It's not real!"

"Stop crying, Mama."

She looked at him with great dark wet eyes. "You had me dancing. We haven't danced in twenty years."

"I'll take you dancing tomorrow night!"

"No, no! It's not important, it *shouldn't* be important. But your machine says it's important! So I believe! It'll be all right, Leo, after I cry some more."

"What else?"

"What else? The machine says, 'You're young.' I'm not. It lies, that Sadness Machine!"

"Sad in what way?"

His wife was quieter now. "Leo, the mistake you made is you

forgot some hour, some day, we all got to climb out of that thing and go back to dirty dishes and the beds not made. While you're in that thing, sure, a sunset lasts forever almost, the air smells good, the temperature is fine. All the things you want to last, last. But outside, the children wait on lunch, the clothes need buttons. And then let's be frank, Leo, how long can you *look* at a sunset? Who *wants* a sunset to last? Who wants perfect temperature? Who wants air smelling good always? So after a while, who would notice? Better, for a minute or two, a sunset. After that, let's have something else. People are like that, Leo. How could you forget?"

"Did I?"

"Sunsets we always liked because they only happen once and go away."

"But Lena, that's sad."

"No, if the sunset stayed and we got bored, that would be a real sadness. So two things you did you should never have. You made quick things go slow and stay around. You brought things faraway to our back yard where they don't belong, where they just tell you, 'No, you'll never travel, Lena Auffmann, Paris you'll never see! Rome you'll *never* visit.' But I *always* knew that, so why tell me? Better to forget and make do, Leo, make do, eh?"

Leo Auffmann leaned against the machine for support. He snatched his burned hand away, surprised.

"So now what, Lena?" he said.

"It's not for me to say. I know only so long as this thing is here I'll want to come out, or Saul will want to come out like he did last night, and against our judgment sit in it and look at all those places so faraway and every time we will cry and be no fit family for you."

"I don't understand," he said, "how I could be so wrong. Just let me check to see what you say is true." He sat down inside the machine. "You won't go away?"

His wife nodded. "We'll wait, Leo."

He shut the door. In the warm darkness he hesitated, pressed the button, and was just relaxing back in color and music, when he heard someone screaming.

"Fire, Papa! The machine's on fire!"

Someone hammered the door. He leaped up, bumped his head, and fell as the door gave way and the boys dragged him out. Behind him he heard a muffled explosion. The entire family was running now. Leo Auffmann turned and gasped, "Saul, call the fire department!"

Lena Auffmann caught Saul as he ran. "Saul," she said. "Wait."
There was a gush of flame, another muffled explosion. When the
machine was burning very well indeed, Lena Auffmann nodded.
"All right, Saul," she said. "Run call the fire department."

Everybody who was anybody came to the fire. There was
Grandpa Spaulding and Douglas and Tom and most of the
boarders and some of the old men from across the ravine and
all the children from six blocks around. And Leo Auffmann's
children stood out front, proud of how fine the flames looked
jumping from the garage roof.

Grandfather Spaulding studied the smoke ball in the sky and
said, quietly, "Leo, was that it? Your Happiness Machine?"

"Some year," said Leo Auffmann, "I'll figure it and tell you."

Lena Auffmann, standing in the dark now, watched as the
firemen ran in and out of the yard; the garage, roaring, settled
upon itself.

"Leo," she said, "it won't take a year to figure. Look around.
Think. Keep quiet a little bit. Then come tell me. I'll be in the
house, putting books back on shelves, and clothes back in clos-
ets, fixing supper, supper's late, look how dark. Come, children,
help Mama."

When the firemen and the neighbors were gone, Leo Auffmann was left with Grandfather Spaulding and Douglas and
Tom, brooding over the smoldering ruin. He stirred his foot in
the wet ashes and slowly said what he had to say.

"The first thing you learn in life is you're a fool. The last thing
you learn in life is you're the same fool. In one hour, I've done a
lot of thinking. I thought, Leo Auffmann is blind! . . . You want
to see the *real* Happiness Machine? The one they patented a
couple thousand years ago, it still runs, not good all the time,
no! but it runs. It's been here all along."

"But the fire—" said Douglas.

"Sure, the fire, the garage! But like Lena said, it don't take a
year to figure; what burned in the garage don't count!"

They followed him up the front-porch steps.

"Here," whispered Leo Auffmann, "the front window. Quiet,
and you'll see it."

Hesitantly, Grandfather, Douglas, and Tom peered through
the large windowpane.

And there, in small warm pools of lamplight, you could see
what Leo Auffmann wanted you to see. There sat Saul and

Marshall, playing chess at the coffee table. In the dining room Rebecca was laying out the silver. Naomi was cutting paper-doll dresses. Ruth was painting water colors. Joseph was running his electric train. Through the kitchen door, Lena Auffmann was sliding a pot roast from the steaming oven. Every hand, every head, every mouth made a big or little motion. You could hear their faraway voices under glass. You could hear someone singing in a high sweet voice. You could smell bread baking, too, and you knew it was real bread that would soon be covered with real butter. Everything was there and it was working.

Grandfather, Douglas, and Tom turned to look at Leo Auffmann, who gazed serenely through the window, the pink light on his cheeks.

"Sure," he murmured. "There it is." And he watched with now-gentle sorrow and now-quick delight, and at last quiet acceptance, as all the bits and pieces of this house mixed, stirred, settled, poised, and ran steadily again. "The Happiness Machine," he said. "The Happiness Machine."

A moment later he was gone.

Inside, Grandfather, Douglas, and Tom saw him tinkering, make a minor adjustment here, eliminate friction there, busy among all those warm, wonderful, infinitely delicate, forever mysterious, and ever-moving parts.

Then smiling, they went down the steps into the fresh summer night.

from

The Genetics Explosion

Alvin and Virginia Silverstein

IF you listen carefully, you may hear an explosion. It's not the kind that goes BANG! No, it's a different kind—a knowledge explosion. Every day thousands of new facts pour out of laboratories throughout the world. Each day we learn more about the world around us and about ourselves.

Over the next two years, scientists will gain more knowledge than people did in all of human history before you were born. Imagine that! In just two years the mountain of new knowledge will be bigger than the mountain that was built up over many thousands of years. We can already see the results of this knowledge explosion. For example, your pocket calculator is more powerful than the million-dollar computers of thirty years ago.

Things are happening so fast in science these days that it is hard for people to keep up. But there is an important area of science that is moving especially fast: molecular genetics—the study of the chemicals of heredity.

You have probably noticed that you look rather like your parents. Perhaps you have eyes like your mother's or a nose that looks just like your father's. Turning the pages of the family photo album, you can trace resemblances to other relatives—perhaps you inherited your grandfather's chin, or hair just the color of your aunt's when she was young. All these traits have been passed down to you, combined into a new pattern that is uniquely yours.

You started life as a single round cell, too small to be seen without a microscope. Yet that single cell contained a complete set of blueprints for building a person and a detailed instruction manual for day-to-day operation. All this information was neatly tucked away inside 46 tiny rod-shaped structures called chromosomes and spelled out chemically in a substance called *deoxyribonucleic acid* (DNA for short). Portions of this DNA, called genes, contain the information needed to produce hormones, enzymes, and other important body chemicals, and to determine traits such as blue eyes, brown hair, and a turned-up nose.

The single cell that was the start of you carefully duplicated its hereditary information, chemical by chemical. Then it divided to form two identical cells, each with a complete set of your own, unique DNA molecules. The two new cells divided in turn, again and again. Gradually, different-looking cells appeared and formed the different parts of your body—brain, heart, eyes, skin, muscles, and so on. Yet before dividing, each cell made its own careful copy of your hereditary information. So even now, each of your trillions of cells has its own complete set of instructions for building your whole body!

Only a small fraction of the DNA in any particular cell is actually working, translating particular instructions into materials to be used for building or maintaining the body. This working DNA contains the instructions needed for that cell's own jobs. The rest of the cell's DNA is "turned off." It is there, and if the cell divides, all of the DNA will be faithfully duplicated and passed on to the new "daughter cells." But most of the DNA isn't doing anything. Imagine the mix-ups that would occur if this were not the case. You might find yourself growing toenails on your eyelids, or eyes on your elbows!

Ideally, each person comes into the world with a set of chemical blueprints for building a strong, healthy body and keeping it that way throughout a long life. But mistakes can happen. Sometimes errors occur in copying the cell's DNA. This doesn't happen very often, but think of how many times cells must divide in order to go from the single cell that starts off a baby to the trillions of cells in the body of an adult. DNA may also be altered by radiations or chemicals. With so many opportunities for changes, it's not surprising that scientists estimate we each are carrying from three to eight *mutations,* or changes, in our genes. Many of these mutations have no apparent effect on us, but there are more than two thousand different genetic diseases known to be the result of something wrong with the chromosomes.

Disease and accidents can also damage the body, leading to illness, disability, and death. If a person loses an arm in an auto accident or has a lung destroyed by cancer, theoretically the healthy cells that remain have all the blueprints needed to build a replacement arm or lung. But they don't do it. The genes for building new arms and lungs are turned off very early in a person's development—long before birth—after the organs of the body have been formed. In most cases, they are not turned on again.

Wouldn't it be wonderful if we could fix damaged DNA, so that people with genetic diseases could be cured? And if we knew how to turn genes on and off when we wanted to, people could grow their own replacement parts! We can't do either of these things yet. Not too many years ago, the idea that we would *ever* be able to do them seemed to be merely wishful thinking, or "science fiction." But now information about genetics—down to the most fundamental level—is flooding in. We have already learned an enormous amount about what the genes are and how they work, and each day we learn more. Now scientists are beginning to work out practical applications of this genetic knowledge. We have progressed from *genetics,* the science that describes heredity, to *genetic engineering,* the application of genetic knowledge for practical purposes. We are gaining the ability to change the living creatures of our world—and to remake ourselves.

What benefits do scientists speculate that the new genetic knowledge may bring? A quarter of a million American children are born each year with birth defects, which may leave them crippled, disfigured, or mentally retarded. Most of these defects have genetic causes, and with enough knowledge we might be able to prevent them. Errors in genes can also cause metabolic diseases, in which chemical reactions in the body don't work properly. Thousands of chemical reactions go on constantly in our bodies, and they are closely interlinked, each reaction depending on many others. These metabolic disorders can cause illness, retarded development, and death. If we had effective ways of locating the faulty genes and correcting them, we could cure the diseases. We might also be able to build in resistance to infectious diseases caused by bacteria and viruses, and help people to repair their own damaged body parts. Genetic engineers are working on other creatures, too, breeding new varieties of plants, for example, which would grow faster and produce larger crops of more nutritious food. Microorganisms—which are already being grown in huge factories to produce a variety of products, from fermented beverages to antibiotics—could be made to order, giving us vast new supplies of hormones, enzymes, and other important biochemicals.

Some people believe that there is another side to the genetic engineering story—that the new knowledge and techniques scientists are developing may bring not only benefits, but also risks. They fear that the new knowledge may be misused—perhaps on purpose, perhaps accidentally—if we try to do too much, before we know how to do it properly. Recently one area of genetic engineering, recombinant DNA research, has stirred a furious debate. In recombinant DNA techniques, genes from other organisms—often plants and animals—are inserted into bacteria. Some scientists and citizens feared that we might accidentally start a horrifying plague that could wipe out the defenseless inhabitants of our planet. As more has been learned about tinkering with bacterial genes, most of these fears have died down. But other sensational news in areas related to the new genetics research, from the birth of the first "test-tube baby" to the publication of a book that claimed to describe the cloning of a human being, has continued to focus attention on some of the deeper questions that this new research is raising. Do we have the right to tamper with our genes and those of other creatures? Might we seriously unbalance the community of life on our planet which has developed over millions of years of gradual change and evolution? Are we "playing God" when we consider the prospect of remaking ourselves?

The recombinant DNA debate brought the average citizen into a far more active role in scientific decision making than ever before. In Cambridge, Massachusetts, and in other communities, people were suddenly faced with the task of deciding whether it was safe and wise to allow certain new types of genetics research to be conducted—decisions that might ultimately affect the whole world's history. It is likely that this kind of debate will continue as the exploding field of genetics research continues to bring stunning new advances. Now more than ever, we all need to learn more about this new science so that our decisions will be responsible ones.

from
The Giver

Lois Lowry

Chapter 1

IT was almost December, and Jonas was beginning to be frightened. No. Wrong word, Jonas thought. Frightened meant that deep, sickening feeling of something terrible about to happen. Frightened was the way he had felt a year ago when an unidentified aircraft had overflown the community twice. He had seen it both times. Squinting toward the sky, he had seen the sleek jet, almost a blur at its high speed, go past, and a second later heard the blast of sound that followed. Then one more time, a moment later, from the opposite direction, the same plane.

At first, he had been only fascinated. He had never seen aircraft so close, for it was against the rules for Pilots to fly over the community. Occasionally, when supplies were delivered by cargo planes to the landing field across the river, the children rode their bicycles to the riverbank and watched, intrigued, the unloading and then the takeoff directed to the west, always away from the community.

But the aircraft a year ago had been different. It was not a squat, fat-bellied cargo plane but a needle-nosed single-pilot jet. Jonas, looking around anxiously, had seen others—adults as well as children—stop what they were doing and wait, confused, for an explanation of the frightening event.

Then all of the citizens had been ordered to go into the nearest building and stay there. IMMEDIATELY, the rasping voice through the speakers had said. LEAVE YOUR BICYCLES WHERE THEY ARE.

Instantly, obediently, Jonas had dropped his bike on its side on the path behind his family's dwelling. He had run indoors and stayed there, alone. His parents were both at work, and his little sister, Lily, was at the Childcare Center where she spent her after-school hours.

Looking through the front window, he had seen no people: none of the busy afternoon crew of Street Cleaners, Landscape Workers, and Food Delivery people who usually populated the community at that time of day. He saw only the abandoned bikes here and there on their sides; an upturned wheel on one was still revolving slowly.

He had been frightened then. The sense of his own community silent, waiting, had made his stomach churn. He had trembled.

But it had been nothing. Within minutes the speakers had crackled again, and the voice, reassuring now and less urgent, had explained that a Pilot-in-Training had misread his navigational instructions and made a wrong turn. Desperately the Pilot had been trying to make his way back before his error was noticed.

NEEDLESS TO SAY, HE WILL BE RELEASED, the voice had said, followed by silence. There was an ironic tone to that final message, as if the Speaker found it amusing; and Jonas had smiled a little, though he knew what a grim statement it had been. For a contributing citizen to be released from the community was a final decision, a terrible punishment, an overwhelming statement of failure.

Even the children were scolded if they used the term lightly at play, jeering at a teammate who missed a catch or stumbled in a race. Jonas had done it once, had shouted at his best friend, "That's it, Asher! You're released!" when Asher's clumsy error had lost a match for his team. He had been taken aside for a brief and serious talk by the coach, had hung his head with guilt and embarrassment, and apologized to Asher after the game.

Now, thinking about the feeling of fear as he pedaled home along the river path, he remembered that moment of palpable, stomach-sinking terror when the aircraft had streaked above. It was not what he was feeling now with December approaching. He searched for the right word to describe his own feeling.

Jonas was careful about language. Not like his friend, Asher, who talked too fast and mixed things up, scrambling words and phrases until they were barely recognizable and often very funny.

Jonas grinned, remembering the morning that Asher had dashed into the classroom, late as usual, arriving breathlessly in the middle of the chanting of the morning anthem. When the class took their seats at the conclusion of the patriotic hymn, Asher remained standing to make his public apology as was required.

"I apologize for inconveniencing my learning community." Asher ran through the standard apology phrase rapidly, still catching his breath. The Instructor and class waited patiently for his explanation. The students had all been grinning, because they had listened to Asher's explanations so many times before.

"I left home at the correct time but when I was riding along near the hatchery, the crew was separating some salmon. I guess I just got distraught, watching them.

"I apologize to my classmates," Asher concluded. He smoothed his rumpled tunic and sat down.

"We accept your apology, Asher." The class recited the standard response in unison. Many of the students were biting their lips to keep from laughing.

"I accept your apology, Asher," the Instructor said. He was smiling. "And I thank you, because once again you have provided an opportunity for a lesson in language. 'Distraught' is too strong an adjective to describe salmon-viewing." He turned and wrote "distraught" on the instructional board. Beside it he wrote "distracted."

Jonas, nearing his home now, smiled at the recollection. Thinking, still, as he wheeled his bike into its narrow port beside the door, he realized that frightened was the wrong word to describe his feelings, now that December was almost here. It was too strong an adjective.

He had waited a long time for this special December. Now that it was almost upon him, he wasn't frightened, but he was . . . eager, he decided. He was eager for it to come. And he was excited, certainly. All of the Elevens were excited about the event that would be coming so soon.

But there was a little shudder of nervousness when he thought about it, about what might happen.

Apprehensive, Jonas decided. That's what I am.

"Who wants to be the first tonight, for feelings?" Jonas's father asked, at the conclusion of their evening meal.

It was one of the rituals, the evening telling of feelings. Sometimes Jonas and his sister, Lily, argued over turns, over who would get to go first. Their parents, of course, were part of the ritual; they, too, told their feelings each evening. But like all parents—all adults—they didn't fight and wheedle for their turn.

Nor did Jonas, tonight. His feelings were too complicated this evening. He wanted to share them, but he wasn't eager to begin the process of sifting through his own complicated emotions, even with the help that he knew his parents could give.

"You go, Lily," he said, seeing his sister, who was much younger—only a Seven—wiggling with impatience in her chair.

"I felt very angry this afternoon," Lily announced. "My Childcare group was at the play area, and we had a visiting group of Sevens, and they didn't obey the rules at *all.* One of them—a male; I don't know his name—kept going right to the front of the line for the slide, even though the rest of us were all waiting. I felt so angry at him. I made my hand into a fist, like this." She held up a clenched fist and the rest of the family smiled at her small defiant gesture.

"Why do you think the visitors didn't obey the rules?" Mother asked.

Lily considered, and shook her head. "I don't know. They acted like . . . like . . ."

"Animals?" Jonas suggested. He laughed.

"That's right," Lily said, laughing too. "Like animals." Neither child knew what the word meant, exactly, but it was often used to describe someone uneducated or clumsy, someone who didn't fit in.

"Where were the visitors from?" Father asked.

Lily frowned, trying to remember. "Our leader told us, when he made the welcome speech, but I can't remember. I guess I wasn't paying attention. It was from another community. They had to leave very early, and they had their midday meal on the bus."

Mother nodded. "Do you think it's possible that their rules may be different? And so they simply didn't know what your play area rules were?"

Lily shrugged, and nodded. "I suppose."

"You've visited other communities, haven't you?" Jonas asked. "My group has, often."

Lily nodded again. "When we were Sixes, we went and shared a whole school day with a group of Sixes in their community."

"How did you feel when you were there?"

Lily frowned. "I felt strange. Because their methods were different. They were learning usages that my group hadn't learned yet, so we felt stupid."

Father was listening with interest. "I'm thinking, Lily," he said, "about the boy who didn't obey the rules today. Do you think it's possible that he felt strange and stupid, being in a new place with rules that he didn't know about?"

Lily pondered that. "Yes," she said, finally.

"I feel a little sorry for him," Jonas said, "even though I don't even know him. I feel sorry for anyone who is in a place where he feels strange and stupid."

"How do you feel now, Lily?" Father asked. "Still angry?"

"I guess not," Lily decided. "I guess I feel a little sorry for him. And sorry I made a fist." She grinned.

Jonas smiled back at his sister. Lily's feelings were always straightforward, fairly simple, usually easy to resolve. He guessed that his own had been, too, when he was a Seven.

He listened politely, though not very attentively, while his father took his turn, describing a feeling of worry that he'd had that day at work: a concern about one of the newchildren who wasn't doing well. Jonas's father's title was Nurturer. He and the other Nurturers were responsible for all the physical and emotional needs of every newchild during its earliest life. It was a very important job, Jonas knew, but it wasn't one that interested him much.

"What gender is it?" Lily asked.

"Male," Father said. "He's a sweet little male with a lovely disposition. But he isn't growing as fast as he should, and he doesn't sleep soundly. We have him in the extra care section for supplementary nurturing, but the committee's beginning to talk about releasing him."

"Oh, *no*," Mother murmured sympathetically. "I know how sad that must make you feel."

Jonas and Lily both nodded sympathetically as well. Release of newchildren was always sad, because they hadn't had a chance to enjoy life within the community yet. And they hadn't done anything wrong.

There were only two occasions of release which were not punishment. Release of the elderly, which was a time of celebration for a life well and fully lived; and release of a newchild, which always brought a sense of what-could-we-have-done. This was especially troubling for the Nurturers, like Father, who felt they had failed somehow. But it happened very rarely.

"Well," Father said, "I'm going to keep trying. I may ask the committee for permission to bring him here at night, if you don't mind. You know what the night-crew Nurturers are like. I think this little guy needs something extra."

"Of course," Mother said, and Jonas and Lily nodded. They had heard Father complain about the night crew before. It was a lesser job, night-crew nurturing, assigned to those who lacked the interest or skills or insight for the more vital jobs of the daytime hours. Most of the people on the night crew had not even been given spouses because they lacked, somehow, the essential capacity to connect to others, which was required for the creation of a family unit.

"Maybe we could even keep him," Lily suggested sweetly, trying to look innocent. The look was fake, Jonas knew; they all knew.

"Lily," Mother reminded her, smiling, "you know the rules."

Two children—one male, one female—to each family unit. It was written very clearly in the rules.

Lily giggled. "Well," she said, "I thought maybe just this once."

Next, Mother, who held a prominent position at the Department of Justice, talked about her feelings. Today a repeat offender had been brought before her, someone who had broken the rules before. Someone who she hoped had been adequately and fairly punished, and who had been restored to his place: to his job, his home, his family unit. To see him brought before her a second time caused her overwhelming feelings of frustration and anger. And even guilt, that she hadn't made a difference in his life.

"I feel frightened, too, for him," she confessed. "You know that there's no third chance. The rules say that if there's a third transgression, he simply has to be released." Jonas shivered. He knew it happened. There was even a boy in his group of Elevens whose father had been released years before. No one ever mentioned it; the disgrace was unspeakable. It was hard to imagine.

Lily stood up and went to her mother. She stroked her mother's arm.

From his place at the table, Father reached over and took her hand. Jonas reached for the other.

One by one, they comforted her. Soon she smiled, thanked them, and murmured that she felt soothed.

The ritual continued. "Jonas?" Father asked. "You're last, tonight."

Jonas sighed. This evening he almost would have preferred to keep his feelings hidden. But it was, of course, against the rules.

"I'm feeling apprehensive," he confessed, glad that the appropriate descriptive word had finally come to him.

"Why is that, son?" His father looked concerned.

"I know there's really nothing to worry about," Jonas explained, "and that every adult has been through it. I know you have, Father, and you too, Mother. But it's the Ceremony that I'm apprehensive about. It's almost December."

Lily looked up, her eyes wide. "The Ceremony of Twelve," she whispered in an awed voice. Even the smallest children—Lily's age and younger—knew that it lay in the future for each of them.

"I'm glad you told us of your feelings," Father said.

"Lily," Mother said, beckoning to the little girl, "Go on now and get into your nightclothes. Father and I are going to stay here and talk to Jonas for a while."

Lily sighed, but obediently she got down from her chair. "Privately?" she asked.

Mother nodded. "Yes," she said, "this talk will be a private one with Jonas."

Chapter 2

JONAS watched as his father poured a fresh cup of coffee. He waited.

"You know," his father finally said, "every December was exciting to me when I was young. And it has been for you and Lily, too, I'm sure. Each December brings such changes."

Jonas nodded. He could remember the Decembers back to when he had become, well, probably a Four. The earlier ones were lost to him. But he observed them each year, and he remembered Lily's earliest Decembers. He remembered when his family received Lily, the day she was named, the day that she had become a One.

The Ceremony for the Ones was always noisy and fun. Each December, all the newchildren born in the previous year turned One. One at a time—there were always fifty in each year's group, if none had been released—they had been brought to the stage by the Nurturers who had cared for them since birth. Some were already walking, wobbly on their unsteady legs; others were no more than a few days old, wrapped in blankets, held by their Nurturers.

"I enjoy the Naming," Jonas said.

His mother agreed, smiling. "The year we got Lily, we knew, of course, that we'd receive our female, because we'd made our application and been approved. But I'd been wondering and wondering what her name would be."

"I could have sneaked a look at the list prior to the ceremony," Father confided. "The committee always makes the list in advance, and it's right there in the office at the Nurturing Center.

"As a matter of fact," he went on, "I feel a little guilty about this. But I *did* go in this afternoon and looked to see if this year's Naming list had been made yet. It was right there in the office, and I looked up number Thirty-six—that's the little guy I've been concerned about—because it occurred to me that it might enhance his nurturing if I could call him by a name. Just privately, of course, when no one else is around."

"Did you find it?" Jonas asked. He was fascinated. It didn't seem a terribly important rule, but the fact that his father had broken a rule at all awed him. He glanced at his mother, the one responsible for adherence to the rules, and was relieved that she was smiling.

His father nodded. "His name—if he makes it to the Naming without being released, of course—is to be Gabriel. So I whisper that to him when I feed him every four hours, and during exercise and playtime. If no one can hear me.

"I call him Gabe, actually," he said, and grinned.

"Gabe." Jonas tried it out. A good name, he decided.

Though Jonas had only become a Five the year that they acquired Lily and learned her name, he remembered the excitement, the conversations at home, wondering about her: how she would look, who she would be, how she would fit into their established family unit. He remembered climbing the steps to the stage with his parents, his father by his side that year instead of with the Nurturers, since it was the year that he would be given a newchild of his own.

He remembered his mother taking the newchild, his sister, into her arms, while the document was read to the assembled family units. "Newchild Twenty-three," the Namer had read. "Lily."

He remembered his father's look of delight, and that his father had whispered, "She's one of my favorites. I was hoping for her to be the one." The crowd had clapped, and Jonas had grinned. He liked his sister's name. Lily, barely awake, had waved her small fist. Then they had stepped down to make room for the next family unit.

"When I was an Eleven," his father said now, "as you are, Jonas, I was very impatient, waiting for the Ceremony of Twelve. It's a long two days. I remember that I enjoyed the Ones, as I always do, but that I didn't pay much attention to the other ceremonies, except for my sister's. She became a Nine that year, and got her bicycle. I'd been teaching her to ride mine, even though technically I wasn't supposed to."

Jonas laughed. It was one of the few rules that was not taken very seriously and was almost *always* broken. The children all received their bicycles at Nine; they were not allowed to ride bicycles before then. But almost always, the older brothers and sisters had secretly taught the younger ones. Jonas had been thinking already about teaching Lily.

There was talk about changing the rule and giving the bicycles at an earlier age. A committee was studying the idea. When something went to a committee for study, the people always joked about it. They said that the committee members would become Elders by the time the rule change was made.

Rules were very hard to change. Sometimes, if it was a very important rule—unlike the one governing the age for bicycles—it would have to go, eventually, to The Receiver for a decision. The Receiver was the most important Elder. Jonas had never even seen him, that he knew of; someone in a position of such importance lived and worked alone. But the committee would never bother The Receiver with a question about bicycles; they would simply fret and argue about it themselves for years, until the citizens forgot that it had ever gone to them for study.

His father continued. "So I watched and cheered when my sister, Katya, became a Nine and removed her hair ribbons and got her bicycle," Father went on. "Then I didn't pay much attention to the Tens and Elevens. And *finally*, at the end of the second day, which seemed to go on forever, it was my turn. It was the Ceremony of Twelve."

Jonas shivered. He pictured his father, who must have been a shy and quiet boy, for he was a shy and quiet man, seated with his group, waiting to be called to the stage. The Ceremony of Twelve was the last of the Ceremonies. The most important.

"I remember how proud my parents looked—and my sister, too; even though she wanted to be out riding the bicycle publicly, she stopped fidgeting and was very still and attentive when my turn came.

"But to be honest, Jonas," his father said, "for me there was not the element of suspense that there is with your Ceremony. Because I was already fairly certain of what my Assignment was to be."

Jonas was surprised. There was no way, really, to know in advance. It was a secret selection, made by the leaders of the community, the Committee of Elders, who took the responsibility so seriously that there were never even any jokes made about Assignments.

His mother seemed surprised, too. "How could you have known?" she asked.

His father smiled his gentle smile. "Well, it was clear to me—and my parents later confessed that it had been obvious to them, too—what my aptitude was. I had always loved the new-children more than anything. When my friends in my age group were holding bicycle races, or building toy vehicles or bridges with their construction sets, or—"

"All the things I do with my friends," Jonas pointed out, and his mother nodded in agreement.

"I always participated, of course, because as children we must experience all of those things. And I studied hard in school, as you do, Jonas. But again and again, during free time, I found myself drawn to the newchildren. I spent almost all of my volunteer hours helping in the Nurturing Center. Of course the Elders knew that, from their observation."

Jonas nodded. During the past year he had been aware of the increasing level of observation. In school, at recreation time, and during volunteer hours, he had noticed the Elders watching him and the other Elevens. He had seen them taking notes. He knew, too, that the Elders were meeting for long hours with all of the instructors that he and the other Elevens had had during their years of school.

"So I expected it, and I was pleased, but not at all surprised, when my Assignment was announced as Nurturer," Father explained.

"Did everyone applaud, even though they weren't surprised?" Jonas asked.

"Oh, of course. They were happy for me, that my Assignment was what I wanted most. I felt very fortunate." His father smiled.

"Were any of the Elevens disappointed, your year?" Jonas asked. Unlike his father, he had no idea what his Assignment would be. But he knew that some would disappoint him. Though he respected his father's work, Nurturer would not be his wish. And he didn't envy Laborers at all.

His father thought. "No, I don't think so. Of course the Elders are so careful in their observations and selections."

"I think it's probably the most important job in our community," his mother commented.

"My friend Yoshiko was surprised by her selection as Doctor," Father said, "but she was thrilled. And let's see, there was Andrei—I remember that when we were boys he never wanted to do physical things. He spent all the recreation time he could with his construction set, and his volunteer hours were always on building sites. The Elders knew that, of course. Andrei was given the Assignment of Engineer and he was delighted."

"Andrei later designed the bridge that crosses the river to the west of town," Jonas's mother said. "It wasn't there when we were children."

"There are very rarely disappointments, Jonas. I don't think you need to worry about that," his father reassured him. "And if there are, you know there's an appeal process." But they all laughed at that—an appeal went to a committee for study.

"I worry a little about Asher's Assignment," Jonas confessed. "Asher's such *fun*. But he doesn't really have any serious interests. He makes a game out of everything."

His father chuckled. "You know," he said, "I remember when Asher was a newchild at the Nurturing Center, before he was named. He never cried. He giggled and laughed at everything. All of us on the staff enjoyed nurturing Asher."

"The Elders know Asher," his mother said. "They'll find exactly the right Assignment for him. I don't think you need to worry about him. But, Jonas, let me warn you about something that may not have occurred to you. I know I didn't think about it until after my Ceremony of Twelve."

"What's that?"

"Well, it's the last of the Ceremonies, as you know. After Twelve, age isn't important. Most of us even lose track of how old we are as time passes, though the information is in the Hall of Open Records, and we could go and look it up if we wanted to. What's important is the preparation for adult life, and the training you'll receive in your Assignment."

"I know that," Jonas said. "Everyone knows that."

"But it means," his mother went on, "that you'll move into a new group. And each of your friends will. You'll no longer be spending your time with your group of Elevens. After the Ceremony of Twelve, you'll be with your Assignment group, with those in training. No more volunteer hours. No more recreation hours. So your friends will no longer be as close."

Jonas shook his head. "Asher and I will always be friends," he said firmly. "And there will still be school."

"That's true," his father agreed. "But what your mother said is true as well. There will be changes."

"*Good* changes, though," his mother pointed out. "After my Ceremony of Twelve, I missed my childhood recreation. But when I entered my training for Law and Justice, I found myself with people who shared my interests. I made friends on a new level, friends of all ages."

"Did you still play at all, after Twelve?" Jonas asked.

"Occasionally," his mother replied. "But it didn't seem as important to me."

"I did," his father said, laughing. "I still do. Every day, at the Nurturing Center, I play bounce-on-the-knee, and peek-a-boo, and hug-the-teddy." He reached over and stroked Jonas's neatly trimmed hair. "Fun doesn't end when you become Twelve."

Lily appeared, wearing her nightclothes, in the doorway. She gave an impatient sigh. "This is certainly a very *long* private conversation," she said. "And there are certain people waiting for their comfort object."

"Lily," her mother said fondly, "you're very close to being an Eight, and when you're an Eight, your comfort object will be taken away. It will be recycled to the younger children. You should be starting to go off to sleep without it."

But her father had already gone to the shelf and taken down the stuffed elephant which was kept there. Many of the comfort objects, like Lily's, were soft, stuffed, imaginary creatures. Jonas's had been called a bear.

"Here you are, Lily-billy," he said. "I'll come help you remove your hair ribbons."

Jonas and his mother rolled their eyes, yet they watched affectionately as Lily and her father headed to her sleeping-room with the stuffed elephant that had been given to her as her comfort object when she was born. His mother moved to her big desk and opened her briefcase; her work never seemed to end, even when she was at home in the evening. Jonas went to his own desk and began to sort through his school papers for the evening's assignment. But his mind was still on December and the coming Ceremony.

Though he had been reassured by the talk with his parents, he hadn't the slightest idea what Assignment the Elders would be selecting for his future, or how he might feel about it when the day came.

The Search for the Magic Lake

An Ecuadorian Folk Tale

Genevieve Barlow

LONG ago there was a ruler of the vast Inca Empire who had an only son. This youth brought great joy to his father's heart but also a sadness, for the prince had been born in ill health.

As the years passed the prince's health did not improve, and none of the court doctors could find a cure for his illness.

One night the aged emperor went down on his knees and prayed at the altar.

"O Great Ones," he said, "I am getting older and will soon leave my people and join you in the heavens. There is no one to look after them but my son, the prince. I pray you make him well and strong so he can be a fit ruler for my people. Tell me how his malady can be cured."

The emperor put his head in his hands and waited for an answer. Soon he heard a voice coming from the fire that burned constantly in front of the altar.

"Let the prince drink water from the magic lake at the end of the world," the voice said, "and he will be well."

At that moment the fire sputtered and died. Among the cold ashes lay a golden flask.

But the emperor was much too old to make the long journey to the end of the world, and the young prince was too ill to travel. So the emperor proclaimed that whosoever should fill the golden flask with the magic water would be greatly rewarded.

Many brave men set out to search for the magic lake, but none could find it. Days and weeks passed and still the flask remained empty.

In a valley, some distance from the emperor's palace, lived a poor farmer who had a wife, two grown sons, and a young daughter.

One day the older son said to his father, "Let my brother and me join in the search for the magic lake. Before the moon is new again, we shall return and help you harvest the corn and potatoes."

The father remained silent. He was not thinking of the harvest, but feared for his sons' safety.

When the father did not answer, the second son added, "Think of the rich reward, Father!"

"It is their duty to go," said his wife, "for we must all try to help our emperor and the young prince."

After his wife had spoken, the father yielded.

"Go if you must, but beware of the wild beasts and evil spirits," he cautioned.

With their parents' blessing, and an affectionate farewell from their young sister, the sons set out on their journey.

They found many lakes, but none where the sky touched the water.

Finally the younger brother said, "Before another day has passed we must return to help father with the harvest."

"Yes," agreed the other, "but I have thought of a plan. Let us each carry a jar of water from any lake along the way. We can say it will cure the prince. Even if it doesn't, surely the emperor will give us a small reward for our trouble."

"Agreed," said the younger brother.

On arriving at the palace, the deceitful youths told the emperor and his court that they brought water from the magic lake. At once the prince was given a sip from each of the brothers' jars, but of course he remained as ill as before.

"Perhaps the water must be sipped from the golden flask," one of the high priests said.

But the golden flask would not hold the water. In some mysterious way the water from the jars disappeared as soon as it was poured into the flask.

In despair the emperor called for his magician and said to him, "Can you break the spell of the flask so the water will remain for my son to drink?"

"I cannot do that, your majesty," replied the magician. "But I believe," he added wisely, "that the flask is telling us that we have been deceived by the two brothers. The flask can be filled only with water from the magic lake."

When the brothers heard this, they trembled with fright, for they knew their falsehood was discovered.

So angry was the emperor that he ordered the brothers thrown into chains. Each day they were forced to drink water from their jars as a reminder of their false deed. News of their disgrace spread far and wide.

Again the emperor sent messengers throughout the land pleading for someone to bring the magic water before death claimed him and the young prince.

Súmac, the little sister of the deceitful youths, was tending her flock of llamas when she heard the sound of the royal trumpet. Then came the voice of the emperor's servant with his urgent message from the court.

Quickly the child led her llamas home and begged her parents to let her go in search of the magic water.

"You are too young," her father said. "Besides, look at what has already befallen your brothers. Some evil spirit must have taken hold of them to make them tell such a lie."

And her mother said, "We could not bear to be without our precious Súmac!"

"But think how sad our emperor will be if the young prince dies," replied the innocent child. "And if I can find the magic lake, perhaps the emperor will forgive my brothers and send them home."

"Dear husband," said Súmac's mother, "maybe it is the will of the gods that we let her go."

Once again the father gave his permission.

"It is true," he murmured, "I must think of our emperor."

Súmac was overjoyed, and went skipping out to the corral to harness one of her pet llamas. It would carry her provisions and keep her company.

Meanwhile her mother filled a little woven bag with food and drink for Súmac—toasted golden kernels of corn and a little earthen jar of *chicha*, a beverage made from crushed corn.

The three embraced each other tearfully before Súmac set out bravely on her mission, leading her pet llama along the trail.

The first night she slept, snug and warm against her llama, in the shelter of a few rocks. But when she heard the hungry cry of the puma, she feared for her pet animal and bade it return safely home.

The next night she spent in the top branches of a tall tree, far out of reach of the dreadful puma. She hid her provisions in a hole in the tree trunk.

At sunrise she was aroused by the voices of gentle sparrows resting on a nearby limb.

"Poor child," said the oldest sparrow, "she can never find her way to the lake."

"Let us help her," chorused the others.

"Oh please do!" implored the child, "and forgive me for intruding in your tree."

"We welcome you," chirped another sparrow, "for you are the same little girl who yesterday shared your golden corn with us."

117

"We shall help you," continued the first sparrow, who was the leader, "for you are a good child. Each of us will give you a wing feather, and you must hold them all together in one hand as a fan. The feathers have magic powers that will carry you wherever you wish to go. They will also protect you from harm."

Each sparrow then lifted a wing, sought out a special feather hidden underneath, and gave it to Súmac. She fashioned them into the shape of a little fan, taking the ribbon from her hair to bind the feathers together so none would be lost.

"I must warn you," said the oldest sparrow, "that the lake is guarded by three terrible creatures. But have no fear. Hold the magic fan up to your face and you will be unharmed."

Súmac thanked the birds over and over again. Then, holding up the fan in her chubby hands, she said politely, "Please, magic fan, take me to the lake at the end of the world."

A soft breeze swept her out of the top branches of the tree and through the valley. Then up she was carried, higher and higher into the sky, until she could look down and see the great mountain peaks covered with snow.

At last the wind put her down on the shore of a beautiful lake. It was, indeed, the lake at the end of the world, for, on the opposite side from where she stood, the sky came down so low it touched the water.

Súmac tucked the magic fan into her waistband and ran to the edge of the water. Suddenly her face fell. She had left everything back in the forest. What could she use for carrying the precious water back to the prince?

"Oh, I do wish I had remembered the jar!" she said, weeping.

Suddenly she heard a soft thud in the sand at her feet. She looked down and discovered a beautiful golden flask—the same one the emperor had found in the ashes.

Súmac took the flask and kneeled at the water's edge. Just then a hissing voice behind her said, "Get away from my lake or I shall wrap my long, hairy legs around your neck."

Súmac turned around. There stood a giant crab as large as a pig and as black as night.

With trembling hands the child took the magic fan from her waistband and spread it open in front of her face. As soon as the crab looked at it, he closed his eyes and fell down on the sand in a deep sleep.

Once more Súmac started to fill the flask. This time she was startled by a fierce voice bubbling up from the water.

"Get away from my lake or I shall eat you," gurgled a giant green alligator. His long tail beat the water angrily.

Súmac waited until the creature swam closer. Then she held up the fan. The alligator blinked. He drew back. Slowly, quietly, he sank to the bottom of the lake in a sound sleep.

Before Súmac could recover from her fright, she heard a shrill whistle in the air. She looked up and saw a flying serpent. His skin was red as blood. Sparks flew from his eyes.

"Get away from my lake or I shall bite you," hissed the serpent as it batted its wings around her head.

Again Súmac's fan saved her from harm. The serpent closed his eyes and drifted to the ground. He folded his wings and coiled up on the sand. Then he began to snore.

Súmac sat for a moment to quiet herself. Then, realizing that the danger was past, she sighed with great relief.

"Now I can fill the golden flask and be on my way," she said to herself.

When this was done, she held the flask tightly in one hand and clutched the fan in the other.

"Please take me to the palace," she said.

Hardly were the words spoken, when she found herself safely in front of the palace gates. She looked at the tall guard.

"I wish to see the emperor," Súmac uttered in trembling tones.

"Why, little girl?" the guard asked kindly.

"I bring water from the magic lake to cure the prince."

The guard looked down at her in astonishment.

"Come!" he commanded in a voice loud and deep as thunder.

In just a few moments Súmac was led into a room full of sadness. The emperor was pacing up and down in despair. The prince lay motionless on a huge bed. His eyes were closed and his face was without color. Beside him knelt his mother, weeping.

Without wasting words, Súmac went to the prince and gave him a few drops of magic water. Soon he opened his eyes. His cheeks became flushed. It was not long before he sat up in bed. He drank some more.

"How strong I feel!" the prince cried joyfully.

The emperor and his wife embraced Súmac. Then Súmac told them of her adventurous trip to the lake. They praised her courage. They marveled at the reappearance of the golden flask and at the powers of the magic fan.

"Dear child," said the emperor, "all the riches of my empire are not enough to repay you for saving my son's life. Ask what you will and it shall be yours."

"Oh, generous emperor," said Súmac timidly, "I have but three wishes."

"Name them and they shall be yours," urged the emperor.

"First, I wish my brothers to be free to return to my parents. They have learned their lesson and will never be false again. I know they were only thinking of a reward for my parents. Please forgive them."

"Guards, free them at once!" ordered the emperor.

"Secondly, I wish the magic fan returned to the forest so the sparrows may have their feathers again."

This time the emperor had no time to speak. Before anyone in the room could utter a sound, the magic fan lifted itself up, spread itself wide open, and floated out the window toward the woods. Everyone watched in amazement. When the fan was out of sight, they applauded.

"What is your last wish, dear Súmac?" asked the queen mother.

"I wish that my parents be given a large farm and great flocks of llamas, vicuñas, and alpacas, so they will not be poor any longer."

"It will be so," said the emperor, "but I am sure your parents never considered themselves poor with so wonderful a daughter."

"Won't you stay with us in the palace?" ventured the prince.

"Yes, stay with us!" urged the emperor and his wife. "We will do everything to make you happy."

"Oh thank you," said Súmac blushing happily, "but I must return to my parents and to my brothers. I miss them as I know they have missed me. They do not even know I am safe, for I came directly to your palace."

The royal family did not try to detain Súmac any longer.

"My own guard will see that you get home safely," said the emperor.

When she reached home, she found that all she had wished for had come to pass: her brothers were waiting for her with their parents; a beautiful house and huge barn were being constructed; her father had received a deed granting him many acres of new, rich farmland.

Súmac ran into the arms of her happy family.

At the palace, the golden flask was never empty. Each time it was used, it was refilled. Thus the prince's royal descendants never suffered ill health and the kingdom remained strong.

But it is said that when the Spanish conqueror of the ancient

Incas demanded a room filled with golden gifts, the precious flask was among them. Whatever happened to this golden treasure is unknown, for the conqueror was killed and the Indians wandered over the mainland in search of a new leader. Some say the precious gifts—including the golden flask—are buried at the bottom of the lake at the end of the world, but no one besides Súmac has ever ventured to go there.

The White-Hair Waterfall

A Chinese Folk Tale

M. A. Jagendorf and Virginia Weng

HIGH up where the Tung people live, there is a mountain called Tou-kao Shan, which means "The Steep High Mountain." Midway to the peak of this mountain a rushing waterfall comes cascading down, looking like white hair flowing over someone's shoulder. The waterfall brings clear sweet water to those who live in the village nearby and to birds and beasts as well. It brings refreshing pleasure to all. Folks call it the White-Hair Waterfall and from it floats a strange tale that happened in the dim far years.

Long ago there were no streams on that mountain, and the people had to wait for the rains from Heaven to give them the much-needed water; and when the heat of the sun dried up the Heaven, folks had to travel full seven *li* to get it.

Now, in the village at the foot of that high peak lived a girl who had the longest hair anyone had ever seen. It was beautiful blue-black in color and reached nearly to her ankles. She would pile most of it on top of her head, and what was still left she would wind around her neck and shoulders, often using it almost as a cloak. The villagers called her the "Long-Hair Girl."

She lived with her old mother who could not walk. Long-Hair Girl took good care of her and of their home. She worked hard in the house and in the garden and in the field, finding food for the young pigs they kept.

One day, while looking for plants to feed the pigs, she walked high up on the mountain and noticed some long, thick, jagged radish leaves growing out among the rocks.

"Those will make a fine meal for my pigs," she said aloud. She began tugging at the leaves and soon out came a big red radish, and from the hole made there gushed out a stream of clear fresh water.

She was thirsty, so she took a long drink. It tasted sweet, and she drank for a long time. When she was through she heaved a deep sigh of pleasure. At the same moment a strong wind came up, whipped the radish out of her hand, and plugged it into the hole from which the water had gushed, closing it tight.

The wind became stronger and lifted the girl and carried her along the peak, setting her down at an opening that led to a cave. She looked around and soon she saw a man all covered with yellow hair sitting on the ground. He looked angry.

"Long-Hair Girl," he said in a deep voice, "you have learned the secret of my sweet-water spring! I am the Spirit of the Mountain, and this spring is mine; I have guarded it for many years. Now you know it. Keep it secret. If you tell anyone, you will lose your life. Remember that!"

Again, the wind blew strongly, lifted Long-Hair Girl from the mouth of the cave, and carried her to her village in front of her home.

She did not tell anyone the secret of the spring. When she saw friends and neighbors struggling on the rocky roads, carrying heavy buckets on shoulder poles to bring precious water from the little river seven *li* away, her heart was filled with pity and sorrow. She could not eat or sleep. She fell silent and her pink cheeks paled. Her beautiful blue-black hair that was the pride of her life turned snow white.

One day she saw an old man struggling over rocks with two buckets of water he had carried a long way. Suddenly the old man's foot hit a boulder and he fell. The buckets dropped from his shoulder pole and turned over, spilling all the precious water. The old man's hand and face were cut and bleeding.

The sight was too much for Long-Hair Girl. Her heart was filled with black misery. She forgot all warning of danger from the yellow-haired Spirit of the Mountain.

"Don't worry about your lost water, Grandfather!" she cried. "There is all the water you need right nearby, right here on the mountainside near our village. I will take you to it. It is guarded jealously by the Spirit of the Mountain, but I know the secret and I will tell it to you and the whole village, though it be my death!"

Having revealed the secret, she felt suddenly relieved. She ran all over the village, shouting, "Come, follow me! All you have to do is pull out the radish and destroy it. There is a spring on the Steep High Mountain! I saw it with my own eyes!" She began running up the mountain to the place where the big radish leaves sprouted. The old man and some neighbors who were near followed her.

She came to the jagged leaves. "Come," she cried, "help me pull out the radish and chop it up quickly!"

They all pulled with a good will and soon the big red radish came out, and with it . . . a stream of cool fresh water.

"Quick!" she cried. "Cut the radish to pieces so that it cannot close the spring again. Quick!" Everyone went at it with his kitchen knife, rock, or stick, while the water kept on flowing.

"Now," she added, "make the opening wide and more water will flow." They all did this with their hands and whatever tools they had. A great mass of water now rushed from the spring.

But at that moment a wild gust of wind carried Long-Hair Girl away, taking her to the cave where the Spirit of the Mountain covered with yellow hair, sat glowering. He was blazing with anger and shouted fiercely at her:

"You betrayed my secret! I will punish you for it by laying you over the cliff at the spring, so that the ice-cold water will always spill over you, and you will suffer forever."

Long-Hair Girl had lost all fear and she answered courageously, "I am willing to suffer for the sake of my relatives and friends in the village. But I ask one favor: Let me return to my home for a short time to find someone to take care of my old mother!"

"You may go," Spirit of the Mountain answered, "but come back quickly or I will destroy the whole village."

A strong wind came along again and carried Long-Hair Girl to her very home. The story had reached there already, and friends and neighbors wholeheartedly promised to help.

It was hard for Long-Hair Girl to leave her mother, whom she loved dearly. She caressed her over and over, but did not tell her that she would never see her again. She said she was going to visit a friend who lived in the next village and she might not come back for a long time.

She petted her little pigs whom she had been feeding, and when she walked up the mountain and passed her favorite banyan tree under which she had rested so often, she stopped and patted the trunk with her hands and said with tears in her voice, "Never again will I rest in your generous shade, my lovely tree!"

At those words a tall old man came from behind the tree. He had green hair and a green beard and his clothes were all deep green too.

"Lovely Long-Hair Girl," he said, "where are you going and why are you crying?" Long-Hair Girl was silent. She sighed and hung her head.

The old man said, "I already know about you. For your kind thoughts and good deed I will save you! I knew you would come this way. Now, look what I have done." He pulled from under the leaves a stone statue that was the image of Long-Hair Girl except for one thing—it had no hair on the head.

"I made it, and now I will take the white hair from your head and put it on the stone head. The Spirit of the Mountain will believe it is you, but it will be the stone statue that will take the eternal punishment of cold water instead."

Long-Hair Girl took the white hair from her head and put it on the stone head where it took root at once.

The tall old man in green lifted the stone statue and took it up the mountain to the spring. There he laid it face downward so that the cold water fell over the long white hair, making of it a long white waterfall.

Suddenly Long-Hair Girl felt a strange prickling on her head . . . where the white hair had been there was a new growth of blue-black hair such as she had had before!

She found herself standing under her beloved banyan tree from which the man in green had come to help her by the power of his magic. He was not there, but his voice came from the tree: "Go home, Long-Hair Girl. Go to your mother whom you love and to your friends for whom you were ready to give your life. Go to them to share their joy and happiness."

And she did just that.

How Old Are You?

H. S. Fritsch

Age is a quality of mind.
If you have left your dreams behind,
  If hope is cold,
If you no longer look ahead,
If your ambitions' fires are dead—
  Then you are old.

But if from life you take the best,
And if in life you keep the jest,
  If love you hold;
No matter how the years go by,
No matter how the birthdays fly—
  You are not old.

Acknowledgments *(continued from p. ii)*

Simon & Schuster Books for Young Readers, as imprint of Simon & Schuster Children's Publishing Division.
Excerpt from *The Genetics Explosion* by Alvin and Virginia Silverstein. Text copyright © 1980 by Alvin and Virginia Silverstein. All rights reserved. Reprinted by permission.

Eiko Tien, Anthony Ramirez and Barbara Mendez for the estate of Genevieve Barlow.
"The Search for the Magic Lake" from *Latin American Tales* by Genevieve Barlow. Copyright © 1966. Reprinted by permission of Eiko Tien, Anthony Ramirez and Barbara Mendez for the estate of Genevieve Barlow.

Vanguard Press, a division of Random House, Inc.
"The White-Hair Waterfall" from *The Magic Boat and Other Chinese Folk Stories* by M. A. Jagendorf and Virginia Weng. Copyright © 1980 by M. A. Jagendorf and Virginia Weng. Reprinted by permission of Vanguard Press, a division of Random House, Inc.

Note: Every effort has been made to locate the copyright owner of material reprinted in this book. Omissions brought to our attention will be corrected in subsequent editions.